HEART of a SAMURAI

BASED ON THE TRUE STORY OF MANJIRO NAKAHAMA

Margi Preus

AMULET BOOKS
NEW YORK

The Library of Congress has catalogued the hardcover edition
of this book as follows:
Preus, Margi.

Heart of a samurai / by Margi Preus.
p. cm.

Summary: In 1841, rescued by an American whaler after a terrible shipwreck leaves him and his four companions castaways on a remote island, fourteen-year-old Manjiro, who dreams of becoming a samurai, learns new laws and customs as he becomes the first Japanese person to set foot in the United States.

ISBN 978-0-8109-8981-8 (alk. paper)

1. Nakahama, Manjiro, 1827–1898—Juvenile fiction. [1. Nakahama, Manjiro, 1827–1898—Fiction. 2. Japanese—United States—Fiction. 3. Japan—Relations—United States—Fiction. 4. United States—Relations—Japan—Fiction.] I. Title.
PZ7.P92434He 2010
[Fic]—dc22
2009051634

Paperback ISBN: 978-1-4197-0200-6

Illustrations by Manjiro (signed John Mung) are noted as such in the captions. Otherwise, the source is the *Hyoson Kiryaku*, and the illustrations are by Kawada Shoryo or another transcriber of the original volumes. The cover art and the illustrations appearing on pages i–xiii, 23, 24–25, 116–17, 187, 188–89, 245, 246–47, and 302–306 are by Jillian Tamaki.

Book design by Chad W. Beckerman

Originally published in hardcover in 2010 by Amulet Books, an imprint of ABRAMS. This edition published in 2012.

Printed and bound in U.S.A.
22

ABRAMS is represented in the UK and Europe by Abrams & Chronicle Books, 1 West Smithfield, London EC1A 9JU and Média Participations, 57 rue Gaston Tessier, 75166 Paris, France.
abramsandchronicle.co.uk and media-participations.com
info@abramsandchronicle.co.uk

ABRAMS The Art of Books
115 West 18th Street, New York, NY 10011
abramsbooks.com

TO PASHA AND MISHA,

AND ADVENTURERS EVERYWHERE

CONTENTS

PART ONE: THE UNKNOWN

PART TWO: THE BARBARIANS

AWARDS & ACCOLADES

Newbery Honor Book, 2011

ALSC Notable Children's Book List, 2011—Older Readers

Kids' Indie Next List, Autumn 2010—Teen Readers

Publishers Weekly, Best Children's Books of 2010—Fiction

Kirkus Reviews, Best Books for Children and Teens, 2010—Fiction with Great Boy Characters; Historical Fiction

New York Public Library, Children's Books of 2010—Stories for Older Readers

Shelf-Awareness, Top Ten Books of 2010

Capitol Choices, Noteworthy Titles for Children and Teens, 2011—ages 10–14

Asian/Pacific American Award for Children's Literature, 2011

Bank Street College, 2011 Best Children's Books of the Year list—ages 12–14, Historical Fiction

REVIEWS

"A terrific biographical novel." —*Wall Street Journal*

★ "It's a classic fish-out-of-water story (although this fish goes into the water repeatedly), and it's precisely this classic structure that gives the novel the sturdy bones of a timeless tale." —*Booklist*, starred review

★ "A captivating fictionalized (although notably faithful) retelling of the boy's adventures." —*Kirkus Reviews*, starred review

★ "Preus mixes fact with fiction in a tale that is at once adventurous, heartwarming, sprawling, and nerve-racking in its depictions of early anti-Asian sentiment." —*Publishers Weekly*, starred review

★ "Preus places readers in the young man's shoes, whether he is on a ship or in a Japanese prison." —*School Library Journal*, starred review

PART THREE: THE NEW WORLD

PART FOUR: RETURNING

PART FIVE: HOME

HEART *of a* SAMURAI

Bird Island as drawn by John Mung

PART ONE
THE UNKNOWN

I have no parents; I make the heaven and earth my mother and father.

I have no home; I make awareness my dwelling.

I have no life and death; I make the tides of breathing my life and death.

—from the Samurai Creed

1

THE STORM

January 1841 (12th Year of Tempō, Year of the Ox),
off the coast of Shikoku, Japan

Manjiro squinted across the expanse of glittering sea at the line of dark clouds forming on the horizon.

"What lies there," he wondered aloud, "across the sea?"

"Nothing you want to know about," Denzo said, hurrying to hoist the sail. "Barbarians live there. Demons with hairy faces, big noses, and blue eyes!"

As Jusuke steered the boat toward home, the fishermen fell silent. In three days they had not caught a single fish. Their families would go hungry. Manjiro swallowed hard when he thought of the empty rice bin at home.

He took one last glance behind them and noticed something strange. Dark streaks ran like ribbons through the water.

"Excuse me please," he said. "What is that in the water?"

Goemon, a boy not much older than Manjiro, said, "Fish!"

"Mackerel!" the others cried. Denzo quickly steered the boat into waters black with fish as the others baited their hooks.

The fishermen hurried to cast their lines into the water, then pulled them in, each time hauling in a fat mackerel. It was Manjiro's job to pluck the fish off the hooks. His hands bled, but he smiled to see the bottom of the boat swimming with plump, flopping mackerel! Wasn't it lucky he had looked back one more time? Now they would all be dreaming of dinners of steaming fish, and maybe even a little rice.

None of them noticed that dark clouds had swallowed the sky. They didn't notice the waves lapping at the boat. They didn't notice the wind until the sail ruffled, then snapped.

"Is the sail supposed to snap like that?" Manjiro asked, forgetting to apologize for his intrusion as he had been taught.

"Boy," Jusuke said, "stick to your work."

"Does the wind often howl so?" Manjiro squeaked. He knew he should not ask so many questions, but he couldn't help himself.

"Quiet, boy," said Toraemon, one of the older fishermen. "You are a pest. I don't know why Denzo agreed to bring you along. Can't you see there are still fish to catch?"

But no sooner had he said this than the wind began to

roar like a dragon. The sail filled with air and yanked the boat on its side until Denzo released the line. Freed, the sail whipped about, flapping like a wounded bird. Toraemon grabbed the oars and pulled, while Jusuke tried to lower the sail. But the wind beat it against the mast until it was torn into shreds. The wind pushed the sea into great mountains of water; it tore the oars from the men's hands and flung them into the sea; and finally, it snapped the mast, then ripped the rudder away from the boat.

Without a sail, without oars, without a rudder, the boat tossed about on the heaving sea. Then a cold rain came that turned to ice. The fishermen huddled in the bottom of the boat, the rain freezing in sheets to the boat, their clothes, their hair.

Days passed. At first they ate the raw flesh of the fish they had caught, but soon the waves that sloshed over the side of the boat had swept away most of their catch.

Once they came within sight of land. They shouted and hollered, but the wind snatched their voices away. Manjiro's heart sank when he realized that the boat was not drifting toward the island, but away.

"*Kuroshio*," Denzo said. "The Black Current." His voice was as dark as the water that surrounded them. Everyone stared at the wide stripe of indigo water which usually flowed north, toward home. This year, for reasons they did not understand, the current flowed southeast. With no sails, no rudder, no oars, they were at *Kuroshio*'s mercy, steadily dragged toward the vast unknown. How long until they came to the end of the ocean and fell off its edge? Would they encounter the frightening creatures and foreign devils that were said to live and sail in the far reaches of the sea?

Everybody knew about the foreign devils—the barbarians. Did they really exist, Manjiro wondered, or were they just the inventions of adults to get children to behave? Even *he* had told his younger sisters, "Go to sleep—or the barbarians will come and get you!"

But now, in the dark of night, the wind screaming as he bailed bucket after bucket of freezing water out of the boat, images of monsters crowded his imagination. Fanged monsters with long, slashing tails, dagger-sharp horns, and icy blue eyes.

By the eighth day of drifting, all the food and water were gone. The cold had penetrated their bones and the fishermen huddled together, prepared to die.

For a long time, no one spoke. They waited for Denzo, the eldest and the leader, to speak first. At last he said, "I was going to buy my own boat when we got home."

Everyone nodded. It was a pity. The boat to which they clung was a borrowed boat.

Next Toraemon spoke. "I was thinking of getting married."

Everyone nodded again. It was a shame he would never marry.

Then Jusuke said through chattering teeth, "I was just looking forward to a hot bath and a fish dinner!"

"With pickled turnips," added Goemon.

Presented with the thought of food, their stomachs ached more fiercely.

Finally, Manjiro, at age fourteen the youngest and so the last to speak, said, "I had hoped to become a samurai."

Everyone laughed. "In his village the fishermen's children are samurai!" Toraemon said. This made them laugh harder.

"Don't tease him," Denzo said. "Obviously, he is delirious."

Am I? Manjiro wondered. He didn't know why he had said he wanted to be a samurai. It was just what came out of his mouth.

He lay shivering, drifting in and out of fitful sleep, listening to the wind whistling through the oarlocks and the waves *tsk-tsking* disapprovingly against the boat. He had hoped this fishing trip would be a way to redeem himself after his dismal failure in his job husking rice for Imasu-san. He'd thought he'd been so clever to add stones to the grinding machine—

it had taken the husks off the rice so much faster. He hadn't considered that the pebbles and stones might get ground up in the rice, too, making it impossible to eat! Imasu-san had been furious, chasing after Manjiro with a willow stick. Manjiro ran. He ran away rather than face his mother after such a foolish mistake. He would find some other work, he thought. He'd find a job in another village and come home with his pockets full of coins, perhaps! Then he wouldn't be so worthless! Now he only wished he had at least stopped to say good-bye to his mother. He could hear her voice, calling him. Over and over she called out.

Finally, he opened his eyes. It was not his mother calling. The sound was made by a large seabird wheeling high overhead.

A bird! He sat up and shook his friend. "Goemon-chan!" he said. "A bird!"

Goemon opened one eye. "It's a bird, that is true." Goemon closed his eyes again. "*Ahodori*—fool bird . . ."

"But, Goemon-chan!" Manjiro shook him again. "Doesn't a bird mean there could be land nearby?"

"Yes," Goemon sighed. Suddenly his head popped up. "Did you say land?"

The two boys shook the others, and they all stared over the side of the boat at a small, dark line on the horizon. As the boat drifted toward it, the dark line grew into a tall, looming shape: an island.

Their hearts beat a little faster. An island could mean freshwater. It might mean food, maybe shelter.

The shape of the island—a tall, flat-topped mountain—became distinct. And yet not at all distinct. Its outline was blurred, as if the skin of the land quivered!

As they drifted closer, it appeared as if pieces of the island broke off and floated up into the air. Or black specks floated down and joined the land.

"Excuse me for asking, but why does it do that?" Manjiro asked.

The fishermen became uneasy. They had drifted into unknown waters. Perhaps the island was bewitched.

They sat silently as the boat drew closer to the undulating island. Once again, Manjiro thought, his questions had led them into danger.

Then Goemon laughed. He had the sharpest eyes, and he could see what the others could not yet see.

"Birds!" he said. "Thousands of birds!"

Soon they could all see the birds soaring in the air, as well as covering the slopes of the island. There were so many birds, thousands lifting up or settling down, that the very island seemed alive.

This was a stroke of luck! They could eat birds, and if they were all fool birds, they would be easy to catch. Perhaps there would be freshwater, too, and other kinds of food.

But as the sun set behind them, illuminating the island with its final, brightest beams, their hopes faded. A barren rock face loomed ahead of them, without a hint of green anywhere. Worse, boulders rose out of the water like sharp claws ready to tear the boat to pieces. Darkness was falling and the boat rushed steadily on—toward the rocks.

2

THE SAMURAI OF BIRD ISLAND

June 27, 1841 (12th Year of Tempō, Year of the Ox)

Earth. Sky. Wind. Sea.

Sometimes it seemed as if that was all there were. All there ever had been. All there ever would be.

There was this scrap of earth—just a big rock, really. And there was a cave in the rock, which offered shelter. Not warm shelter, but shelter.

There was sky, plenty of sky, all the sky you could want. Day after day it hung like a swath of blue silk, and at night like a black velvet cloak studded with cold jewels. It gave little warmth. And barely any rain.

There was the wind. Howling, growling, moaning, roaring.

And there was the glittering sea.

"Blue as a barbarian's eye," Goemon had said. "I hate the sea." They had been climbing the rocks toward the albatross nests. That was back when the fool birds were easy to catch, because they would not abandon the eggs in their nests. You could just reach out and grab them.

"Goemon-chan!" Manjiro had scolded his friend. "How can you say you hate the sea?"

"I know, I know," Goemon said. "The sea has a powerful *kami*, but look at her! She is so cruel! Nothing but water as far as you can see, yet can we drink even a handful? Full of fish, yet can we catch one? When we get out of here, I'm never going to look at the sea again."

"But you are a fisherman, Goemon-chan," Manjiro had said. "How will you fish, if you never look at the sea?"

"I shall wear a blindfold," he said.

Manjiro laughed.

That was back when they used to laugh. Back when there had been birds, thousands of albatross flopping about on their enormous feet, clacking their bills and flapping their huge wings.

But that was then.

Now Manjiro hung over a rock ledge, groping with his fingers on the underside for any clinging shellfish or strip of seaweed. Something to bring back to the others, who were too weak to leave the cave. With his back to the sky and his belly pressed to the earth, Manjiro stared down into the blue eye of the sea.

The water was so clear, he could see straight to the bottom. A snail was making a path like a shiny ribbon slowly unfurling on the sand. How does a snail move when it has no feet? he wondered. And where was the tiny creature going with such purpose?

Manjiro watched it, losing himself in its slow, graceful movement. He remembered how the days had passed, so many sunrises fading into sunsets, until finally he had lost count.

There had been the first day, of course, the day their little boat had splintered on the rocks. Manjiro, Goemon, and Toraemon dove in just before the boat capsized, but Denzo and Jusuke had been trapped underneath. Eventually, all five made it to shore, but Jusuke's leg was injured in the struggle. Still unhealed, Jusuke never left the cave.

There had been the day the earth shook and rocks tumbled down, blocking the entrance to their shelter. But they had been able, with all of them pushing, to roll the rocks away. That was back when they had enough strength for work like that.

The few days the sky had given up some rain were very good days. Rain pooled in the depressions and cracks in the rock. The fishermen collected water in eggshells and the bucket that had drifted ashore, but nothing held enough to last until the next rain. They rationed their water: one oyster shell per bird eaten. That was back when there had been water. And birds.

There had been so many birds, they had gotten sick of them.

"Oh, for a cucumber!" Goemon had said one day. "A bite of sweet potato! I am soooo sick of raw bird."

But Manjiro had an idea. "Let us cook them today, Goemon," he said.

"Yes, let's, with a nice rich sauce and many spices. . . . ," Goemon teased, but then grew serious. "Manjiro-chan, you know our flint and steel are on the bottom of the sea. We have no fire."

"I've been thinking, though," Manjiro said. "Maybe there's another way."

They skinned the birds as usual, with the fish spears they'd salvaged from the boat wreck. Next, they pounded the bird meat with stones until it turned into a kind of paste.

"Now we'll let the sun bake it," Manjiro said, smearing the paste on a rock. "All we have to do is wait."

While they waited, they stared out across the ocean, toward the northwest—toward home. Manjiro's stomach tightened with worry. How was his family getting along without him? Were his little sisters gathering taro in the mountains, trying to find something to eat? Oh, how he wished he could fly like these birds, wheeling and caterwauling above them! He would fly home to his family; he could take them a fish in his beak!

"Thinking about home?" Goemon said.

Manjiro nodded.

"I guess you'll never become a samurai now, huh, Manjiro-chan?"

"Why not?" Manjiro asked.

"Even if we should get home, you know very well you can't be. You weren't born into a samurai family. You were born a fisherman's son and you will be a fisherman, and any sons you have, they also will be fishermen. That is the way it is; that is the way it has always been; that is the way it will always be."

Manjiro sighed. That was always the reason; that had always been the reason; and, he supposed, that would always be the reason.

"Why would you want to be a samurai anyway? So you could beat up on poor peasants like us?" Goemon asked.

Goemon had probably never actually seen a samurai. Manjiro certainly hadn't. His village was far away from the hub of government and power, where most of the samurai spent their time, but of course he had heard stories. Before Manjiro's father had died, he had taught Manjiro about Bushido, the samurai code of honor.

"I wouldn't be that kind of samurai," Manjiro said. "I'd be like the noble samurai of old times: heroic warriors who were loyal to their lords, and who studied calligraphy and poetry as well as the art of fighting."

"We can never go back to Japan, you know," Goemon said, staring across the sea.

"Why not?"

"The law says, 'Any person who leaves the country and later returns will be put to death.'"

They brooded on this in silence.

Finally, Manjiro said, "But *why*?"

"Because, if we were to encounter any of the foreign devils, we would be poisoned by them."

"Poisoned!" Manjiro said.

"Maybe not our bodies, but they will poison our minds with their way of thinking. That's why no fishermen are allowed to go very far from the coast—they say 'contamination lies beyond the reach of the tides.' The barbarians would fill our heads with wrong thoughts!"

"What kind of wrong thoughts?" Manjiro said.

"Manjiro-chan, you ask too many questions," Goemon said.

"I know," Manjiro said. "I'm sorry." He hung his head, but then looked up again. "I hope the barbarians will never find us. May the gods protect us from them!" he cried. Then he plucked up two pieces of driftwood of unequal length. He bowed to his friend, presenting the smooth, worn sticks in both his outstretched hands.

"Oh, honored friend," he said, "I present your *katana*—your long sword. And your *wakizashi*—your short knife."

Then he took two smooth pieces of driftwood of unequal length for himself. He shoved the short piece into the cloth belt he wore around his waist and waved the other one like a sword, challenging Goemon.

"We can't carry swords," Goemon said. "You know that."

"May I humbly suggest," Manjiro said, "that on this island, *we* are the rulers—we are the Samurai of Bird Island. And from now on we shall live by Bushido. And we shall defend our honor and our island and each other against the blue-eyed barbarians." He leaped up onto a rock and swung his stick over his head. "Agreed?"

Goemon jumped up. "Agreed," he said, jamming his "knife" into his sash and slashing at Manjiro's "sword." Their imaginary swords clashed and clattered as they lunged or leaped aside to avoid being hit.

Manjiro had just knocked Goemon's stick from his hand when he felt his own stick snatched away from him. He turned to see Denzo frowning at them both.

"Do you think this is a picnic?" Denzo barked. "You boys were sent to find water and food, not to play at sword fighting."

The boys quickly bowed to Denzo, then pointed at their meat cooking on the rocks.

Denzo squinted at it. "What is that?" he said.

"Stone roast!" Goemon said.

Manjiro laughed. Even Denzo couldn't help but smile.

After that they made stone roast often. It wasn't delicious, but it was at least different from eating raw bird meat.

That was back when they *had* bird meat, back when the

Drawing of Denzo, Goemon, and Manjiro
(The artist has drawn them much older than they were at the time.)

island had been alive with feather-fluttering, wing-flapping, beak-clacking, mooing, cooing, belly-flopping birds. But in the course of a few months, it had come to an end. The babies that were hatching when the fishermen first landed had grown up. Once they were strong enough, all the birds flew away.

Now the island was utterly still and silent.

One day Manjiro and Denzo had agreed it was worth climbing the big hill to look for water. The two of them clambered up the rocky slope. At the top, Manjiro noticed two oblong piles of stones. He stared at them for a long time thinking that they reminded him of something.

"Denzo-san," Manjiro said. "Excuse me for interrupting your thoughts, but what are—?" he broke off, realizing what the piles of rocks were. "Graves!" The word escaped his mouth.

Denzo chanted, "*Namu Amida Butsu*—Buddha of Infinite Light." They wept to think that people had been here before them, people who had died!

"Where do you think they came from?" Manjiro wondered. "Do you think they were our countrymen?"

Denzo just shook his head, and with heavy steps, they plodded back to the cave. Manjiro thought about never seeing his family again. What would happen to his family without him bringing home fish, a little rice—even the mushrooms and ferns he used to gather in the forests that had helped keep them alive? Would they starve? Would there be graves for all of them, too?

The ache he had felt when his father died had been a sharp pain at first, but had dulled over time until he hardly noticed it. But now, like a sore muscle, the pain flared up again. He longed for his mother, and for his dead father, too. Imagining himself dead in one of those graves made him even miss himself!

When Denzo told the others about what they had seen, the gathering grew solemn.

"That could be our fate," Toraemon said.

"I have thought that also," said Denzo.

Everyone turned to Jusuke, who heard none of this conversation. He tossed and moaned, in the throes of fever.

Tears streamed down their faces. None of them wanted to have to bury any of their friends.

Manjiro felt the darkness about to swallow them. But he pushed it away. He had thought of something.

"Please pardon me, friends," he said softly, "but I have a question."

Toraemon said sharply, "Manjiro, now is not the time—"

But Denzo laid a hand on Toraemon's arm and said to Manjiro, "What is it?"

"There were two graves, right, Denzo-san?" Manjiro said.

Denzo nodded.

"My question is: Where is the third person?"

Everyone stared at Manjiro.

"Who *made* the graves?"

Of course, he was right—someone had to have survived to bury the others.

"Maybe," Manjiro said, brightening, "maybe whoever survived was rescued!"

This idea heartened them; they lay down to sleep a little less burdened.

That night their beds were more comfortable than before—Toraemon and Goemon had salvaged some planks that had washed ashore from their broken boat. So instead of stretching out on cold rock, they each had a wide board on which to sleep.

"Please excuse my intrusion," Manjiro whispered, "but thanks for the planks." When the others chuckled, he smiled. He had pushed aside the darkness for the time being.

Much time had passed since then, and now, hanging over the rock ledge staring at the snail in the water, Manjiro wondered how much longer they could last. There was so very little to eat. There was so little water, they had even tried drinking their own urine. Those rocky graves would not leave his thoughts.

He had not found any shellfish or seaweed clinging to the rock, and he had spent too much time watching the snail. But the snail had created such a beautiful design in the sand, like a *kare-sansui*, a Zen garden. Yet not created, Manjiro realized—*traced*. The snail had taken its long, arduous journey to trace—

"My face!" Manjiro whispered. The shadow of Manjiro's face must have seemed like an island of shade in the bright sea. The snail and I, Manjiro thought, are alike. I trace out the length and breadth of this island every day, pacing around and around its face. Like the snail, I have no idea of all that lies beyond.

Beyond this island was a world about which Manjiro knew nothing. It was, perhaps, a huge world. It might be a frightening place, full of demons and monsters. But it might be a dazzling world, full of wonder and mystery. It might be, he thought, very beautiful. If only he had wings, he could fly across the ocean and see all there was to see. Then he would fly home, his beak full of food, his head full of wonders.

Manjiro stood to look out beyond the edges of his island. But standing up so fast made him dizzy. The sky, the sea, the

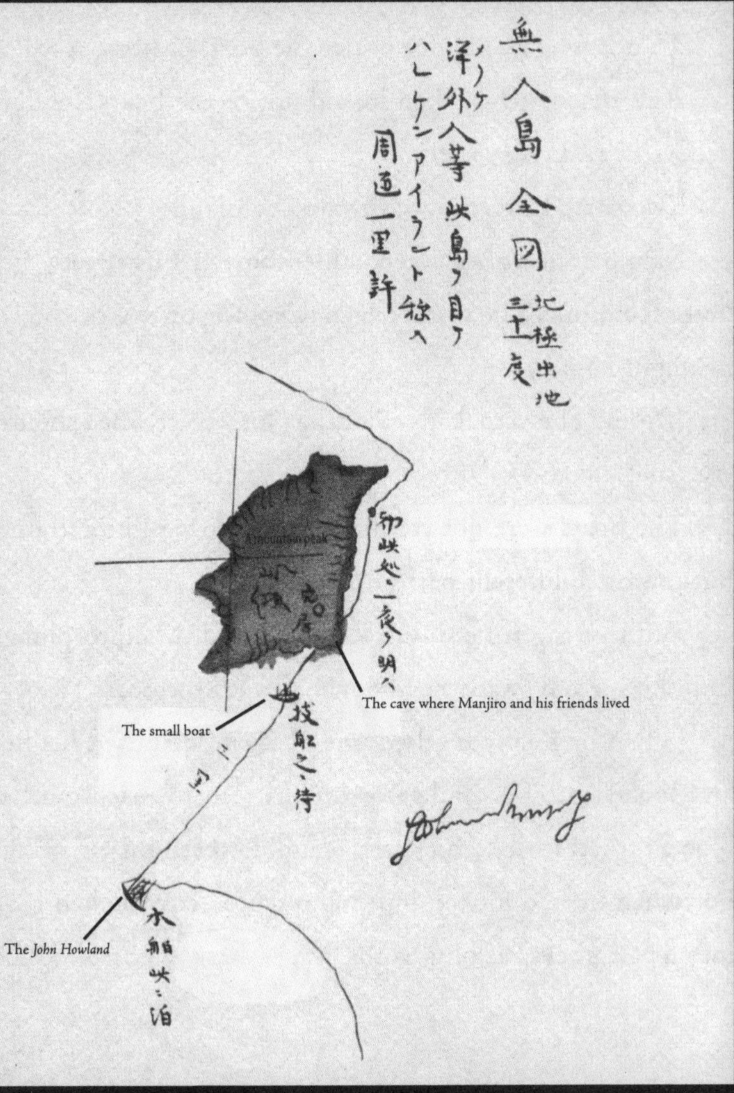

Bird Island as drawn by John Mung

earth all spun around him, in a blur of blue and green and gray, as if he'd been twirling and twirling.

That is why he did not notice the boats at first.

And that is why, when he *did* notice the boats, he didn't believe he really saw them.

Two small boats moved toward the island.

Manjiro's heart beat deep in his stomach. His already weak limbs felt numb. The world began to spin again and he thought he might faint.

"Boats!" he croaked. Finding his voice, he shouted, "Rescue!"

The boats were not coming straight toward him, though, but toward a different part of the island.

With strength he didn't know he had, Manjiro plunged into the sea and swam, head down, toward the boats.

When he finally reached one of them, he raised his head and looked up. He could not lift his arm to reach out. His blood turned to ice, and dizzy again, he felt himself sinking. For when he had looked into his rescuer's face, he had gazed into a pair of eyes as blue as the sea.

Drawing of the *John Howland*

PART TWO
THE BARBARIANS

When meeting difficult situations, one should rush forward bravely and with joy. It is the crossing of a single barrier.

—from *Hagakure: The Book of the Samurai*

3

THE *JOHN HOWLAND*

June 27, 1841

In Japan there was an artist named Hiroshige who made beautiful pictures of everyday scenes. Manjiro had seen some of these prints: two men seeking shelter from rain that fell in cold, slanting streaks; three travelers lighting their pipes by a fire so real it seemed to glow; several geishas in such fine kimonos, you could almost hear the silk rustling.

Forever afterward, when Manjiro thought of what happened that day, he would remember it in sudden, vivid scenes like Hiroshige's prints. And yet unlike those pictures, because nowhere in any of them were there scenes as strange as these:

Twelve shoes, Manjiro counted, as he sat on the bottom of the boat. Stiff-looking things, brown as the skin of hairless dogs. Shiny and smooth, as if made of animal hide.

Manjiro shuddered. These were certainly barbarians if they killed animals to make shoes! Such a thing was against the law in Japan.

Eleven eyes. When at last he dared to look up, what he noticed was their eyes. Each pair a different color: green as a stormy sea, blue as the sky, black as night, or brown as his own. One man had only one eye, and that one as gray as a cloudy day. The other eye was covered with a patch.

There did not seem to be any tails, horns, or fangs among them. There were some alarmingly hairy faces and plenty of big noses, though!

Six big noses, in fact: one long and hooked, two long and straight, one squashed and wide, one turned up at the end, and another as big and red as a radish.

No matter how odd-looking or dangerous they were, Manjiro had to choke down his fear and ask them to help his friends.

"My friends are still on the island," Manjiro said.

But it was clear these creatures didn't understand.

Then Manjiro remembered. It was said the barbarians were simple-minded.

Perhaps if he spoke very slowly. "My . . . friends . . . on . . . island," he said, spacing the words out deliberately.

Beneath the big noses, their mouths spouted gibberish. They don't know how to talk, Manjiro thought—they are just pretending.

Then, there! Along the shore: Toraemon leaped about the

rocks like a monkey. Goemon had tied his tattered tunic on a stick and waved it like a flag.

The foreigners turned their boats and rowed toward shore. Manjiro's heart pounded. What had he done? Had he brought help or certain death? Had he made things worse? What would his friends think when they saw the strange men?

When they got closer, Manjiro saw Goemon's grip shift on his stick. That stick was his *katana*, Manjiro realized, his play sword. He remembered their vow to defend the island against the barbarians.

A glance passed between the two boys, a glance that spoke of gnawing hunger, desperate thirst, endless wind, penetrating cold. Nothing could be worse than staying on this island, the glance said.

Goemon dropped his stick.

The strangers leaped out of their boats and pulled them up on the small beach. By signs, they made it clear the castaways should climb aboard.

The fishermen exchanged frightened glances and whispered to one another, "What about Denzo and Jusuke?"

Gesturing, Manjiro communicated to the strangers about the two men in the cave. Denzo and Jusuke were retrieved, both of them so weak they had to be carried to the boats. Everyone found a place and the sailors shoved off. The two boats rowed away from the island toward an unknown future.

The sun flickered on the restless waves just as it always did. The wind blew just as steadily as it always had. Yet everything had changed. They had been rescued from the island, only to be taken captive by barbarians.

Manjiro stared at the strangers when he thought they weren't looking. Sometimes he caught them staring at him when they thought *he* wasn't looking.

The strange men were all different colors! Their skins were the colors of weathered wood, or clay, white sand, or dried grasses. One was as black as soot! And all different kinds and colors of hair—like the leaves in fall: yellow, red, brown. The black man's head was crowded with tight knots. The head of one man seemed to be covered all over with bright golden coins! All the men were burned and weather-beaten, their faces creased and stained with grime. And they were big. Very big.

As the boats rounded the tip of the island, the fishermen gasped. An enormous bird with many huge, white wings sat upon the water. But, no, it was a ship, bristling with masts, slung with dozens of sails, and alive with movement. Many strange foreigners scurried about on deck or crawled up the ropes that were strung all over the vessel like spiderwebs.

"It's as long as seven of our boats!" Denzo gasped.

"And as wide as eight!" Toraemon whispered.

"Look at all those foreign devils!" Goemon choked on the words.

"Look at all those sails!" Manjiro said. "They are like huge wings!" In a ship like that, he thought, you could go so far and so fast, you could sail clear off the edge of the earth. The thought filled him with both fear and exhilaration.

"We must be very careful how we act," Denzo said.

Roused from his fever, Jusuke whispered, "As the saying goes: 'Entering the village, obey the village.'"

And it *was* like a village, they thought, as they were swept on board the *John Howland* and through a series of small rooms, like tiny houses, each one more ornately decorated than the last.

"Only someone very important could own rooms like these," Goemon whispered.

"A lord."

"A daimyo."

"Maybe even a shogun!" Manjiro gasped.

They found themselves standing before the man who must be the ruler of the ship. He was everything they had heard the foreign devils to be: tall, hairy-faced, with a nose like an albatross's beak. He stood straight as a ship's mast, wearing a stiff, deep blue jacket.

In the brief moment that Manjiro dared to look at this ruler, he saw that the man gazed down at them with one dark eye, while squeezing the other shut. Everything about him seemed concentrated into the steely gaze of this one eye: authority, strength, sadness, and something else Manjiro couldn't name. The fishermen, dizzy and fearful, sank to their knees.

"Captain Whitfield," a sailor called him, and Manjiro tucked away those words before he and the others were whisked off again.

They found themselves seated on benches before a table, with their legs swinging under them.

"You see," Goemon whispered to Manjiro, "the torture has begun."

It wasn't torture, exactly, but it wasn't very comfortable, either.

"Look at your legs hanging there," Goemon said.

"It *is* a strange way to sit!" Manjiro agreed.

"If you were a real samurai, you would commit seppuku now, rather than wait to be humiliated by the barbarians," Goemon said.

"Maybe they won't humiliate us," Manjiro said hopefully.

At this, Goemon simply grunted.

As they sat in this unfamiliar position, with the boat rolling under them, a powerful memory swept over Manjiro. It was so real, it was almost as if it were happening. In the memory, he was at home. Rain tapped lightly on the roof. It must have been a special day because he could smell the sweet perfume of cooking rice. Why, he wondered, did rice have no smell when it was raw, but smelled so heavenly when it was cooking?

He was brought back to the present moment when a bowl of steaming rice was set before him. A real bowl. Of real rice. It had not been a dream. The wonderful, unexpected smell of rice cooking had fanned the embers of memory.

Each of them was also given a metal stick, with four prongs on one end.

"Fork," the sailor said—and showed them they should use it to eat the rice.

The fishermen recited their prayer before eating. "*Itadakimasu*—I will humbly receive."

Then Goemon said, "It might be poison."

"If we're eating poison," Jusuke said, reciting an old proverb, "we might as well lick the plate."

Manjiro didn't care if the rice were poisoned. He gobbled it up gratefully. And the soft, steaming sweet potato. And the warm broth. And the half cup of cool, fresh water. And, finally, a strange kind of food was placed in his hands.

Manjiro bit off a piece. It filled his mouth and made hard work for his teeth.

"Bread," the sailor called it.

• • •

After they ate, their raggedy clothes were taken away and they were given the same strange clothing the sailors wore.

"This will be drafty!" Goemon said, pointing to his shirt flapping open. "This opening will let in a lot of cold air."

One of the sailors pointed out a row of small, round disks on the shirt. He showed them how each disk slipped into a corresponding slit.

"Buttons," the sailor called these closures.

"Buttons," Manjiro repeated to himself. He had never seen

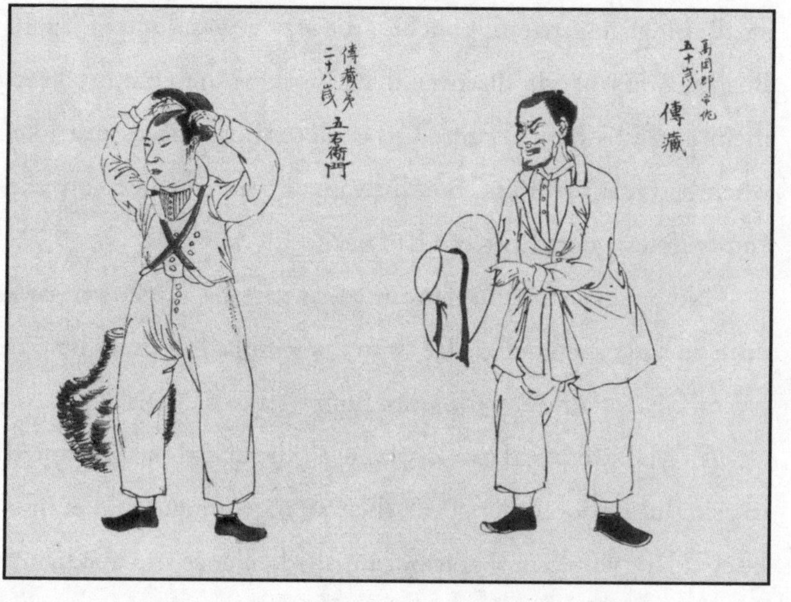

Drawing of Denzo and Goemon in Western clothing

buttons before. None of them had. They were accustomed to tying their clothes together with belts, sashes, or ties.

The boys fumbled with their buttons. Manjiro couldn't help but laugh.

"How can you laugh at a time like this?" Goemon said.

"I am sorry," Manjiro said. He pulled a strange kind of pouch out of his trousers and frowned.

"Pocket," the sailor said. He scooped out the contents of his own pocket—a pebble, a button, a short length of twine—to show them how to use it.

Manjiro wondered why the foreigners didn't just carry their small things in separate pouches, the way it was done in Japan. But once his hands discovered his pockets, he couldn't keep them out. His hands wanted to explore those spaces just like, when he'd lost teeth as a boy, his tongue wanted to explore the empty holes where his teeth had been.

"Now I am sure they mean to torture us," Goemon said, once he had crammed his feet into the stiff leather shoes he was given. "Oh, for a nice, soft pair of floppy straw sandals!"

All Manjiro could think of were all the questions he wanted to ask. But he could not speak their strange tongue, and even if he could, he would probably be punished. Silence and obedience were the safest route to staying alive.

• • •

That night, lying in his bunk, Manjiro couldn't help trying the new words. "Buttons," he whispered. "Pockets. Shoes. Bread." Bread was hard to say. He tried again and again. "Captain," he said. "Whitfield."

"What are you doing?" Goemon said.

"Maybe if I learn some words, I can ask questions."

Goemon groaned. "More questions!"

"If we don't learn their language, how will we know what they intend to do to us?"

"Every time you ask questions, we get into trouble."

"You are right," Manjiro said, "but don't you wonder so many things? Why are there so many barbarians on such a big ship? Why are there so many small boats? What are those big cooking pots for?"

"One of those pots is big enough to fit both of us!" Goemon said.

Manjiro shivered.

Goemon moaned, got up, and went out. He was not accustomed to the motion of such a big vessel. That, combined with his hatred of the sea and his fear of the strangers, made him sick.

When he returned he said, "Manjiro-chan, aren't you afraid? Don't you worry what they will do to us?"

Manjiro was afraid, but he said, "My father told me that a

person should always put his heart in order before falling asleep. Then he will be unencumbered by fear."

Manjiro tried to put his heart in order. He said a sutra—a prayer—for his ancestors, his family, his friends, and for himself. Then he waited for his heart to go back where it belonged instead of jumping all over inside his chest.

Eventually, he must have fallen asleep, for he woke sometime in the night. For a moment he thought he was back in the cave on the island. But everything was very strange. The whole earth seemed to rock beneath him, and there was such eerie creaking and tinging. And what sounded like the growling of wild animals. After a moment he remembered he was on a ship, among foreign men. Snoring foreign men. Smelly foreign men. "Butter stinkers" he'd heard foreigners called. Eating butter made them stink.

Slowly and quietly, he turned his head slightly to look at them, and gasped. A pair of eyes stared back at him from across the space—blue eyes, glittering with menace.

Manjiro squeezed his eyes shut and tried to still his wildly pounding heart. He could not possibly be afraid, he reminded himself, for his heart was in order.

4

THE HUNT

"I still have so many questions. Don't you?" Manjiro said to Goemon one day. They sat near the foremast, where Manjiro was making a sketch of an anchor. "Don't you wonder how they find their way out here in the open ocean, with no landmarks to guide them?"

"Maybe they are just sailing around aimlessly," Goemon answered sullenly. "It seems that way to me."

"Don't you wonder what they're doing, though?"

"All I wonder is when we are going to go home," Goemon said. Weeks had passed, and although they had been sailing north—toward Japan—they still had not caught sight of the lush green hills and rocky coast of their homeland. When they began sailing more westerly, still Manjiro held out hope.

He had found his new pockets to be useful for tucking away scraps of food—a little hardtack, a bit of cheese. One of the sailors had given him a small box in which to keep his few belongings, and every night he emptied his pockets into this box. Then he slid the box under his bunk. When he got home, he planned to give these treasures to his family.

"Why don't you ask them when—or if—we are going home?" Goemon said. "You ask them about everything else."

Manjiro had not been able to keep quiet as he'd intended. Questions just seemed to pop out of him, and he had learned many things. He had learned the words for halyard, windlass, cargo hatch, and ratlines. He could name all sixteen sails, from the spanker to the jibs. But when or whether they were going home was not a question he dared ask. Denzo was the only one with enough authority to talk to the captain.

If only he could summon the courage, Manjiro could ask someone the other question he wondered about most deeply. He nodded his head toward the man posted high on the main mast and said, "There's always someone standing way up there on those little boards. All day, and even at night—if the moon is bright—those fellows stare out at the sea."

"They're looking for something," Goemon said.

"Yes, but what?" Manjiro said.

"Japanese boys," Goemon answered.

"All these small boats. What are they for?"

"To go fetch the Japanese boys when they find them."

"And those big cooking pots on deck. What is their purpose?"

"To cook the Japanese boys."

"If they were going to eat us, why didn't they just do it and get it over with? Why waste their food and water on us?"

"They're fattening us up. We're too skinny."

Manjiro looked Goemon up and down. "Honored friend, I am going to tell you something. You are not too skinny. Not anymore."

"I'm not?" Goemon cried and leaped up to examine his stomach. "Do you think they will eat me?"

"No," Manjiro said. "You would be too sour. Listen, Goemon-chan, I am going to find out what they're doing. I am going to ask the first person I see." He stood up and brushed off his trousers.

"Well, you are going to get yourself into trouble with all those questions. . . ." Goemon's voice trailed off and Manjiro looked up.

Captain Whitfield loomed above him, his one squinting eye trained on Manjiro.

Manjiro gulped. He shouldn't bother such an important man! He bowed deeply and waited for the captain to speak.

"What is it? Out with it—smartly, now!"

Manjiro swallowed hard and began, "Sorry for bother you . . ."

"Boy!" Captain Whitfield said sharply, and Manjiro ducked his head. Goemon had been right. He had been impertinent and would be punished.

Captain Whitfield circa 1865

"Stop apologizing for asking questions!" the captain said. "How are you going to learn if you don't ask things? Ask all the questions you like whenever you like to whomever you like." The captain tipped Manjiro's chin up and looked him in the eye. "Do you understand?"

Manjiro began to bow, but the captain put his hand on his shoulder.

"One other thing," he said. "It is good to be respectful, but it would be well if you would stop that incessant bowing!"

Manjiro glanced at Goemon and realized Goemon had no idea what the captain had said. Manjiro hadn't understood *everything,* but he did understand that the captain wanted him to ask questions. He encouraged it! Manjiro could ask all the questions he wanted, whenever he wanted, to whomever he wanted. The captain had said so.

Manjiro felt he needed a moment to wonder at this. He ran to his favorite hiding spot—one of the small boats suspended from the side of the ship. He scrambled up and over the side and sat on the bottom of the boat, hugging himself as if he'd just been given a gift. But a gift from a barbarian! He shivered. Perhaps it would be better if he stayed away from these strangers.

His thoughts were interrupted by a hearty shout from the

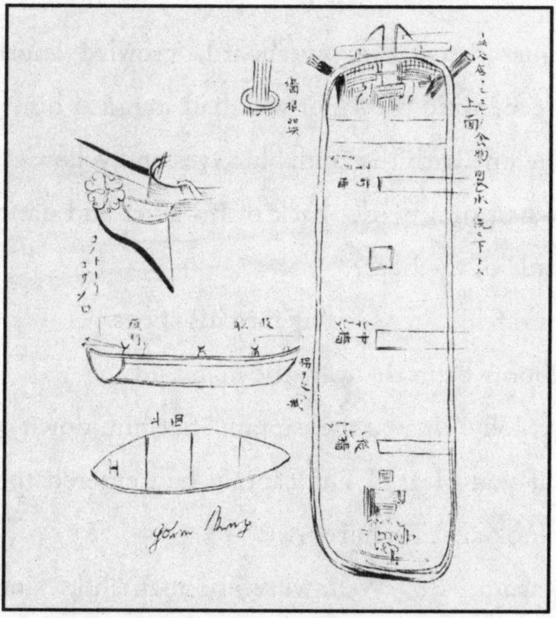

John Mung's drawings of the *John Howland*

sailor posted on the mainmast. The sailor pointed at something far away. Finally, Manjiro thought, he has seen what he was looking for. Land?

Suddenly the deck was alive with the scuffling of many feet. Everyone on deck! Everyone busy! And yet in a strangely hushed and quiet way. Orders were given in husky whispers; after that first shout, there were no more loud voices.

Before Manjiro had time to clamber out, the boat in which he hid was lowered into the water, and sailors scrambled down the ropes and into it. As there was nowhere to hide, Manjiro was quickly discovered.

"Eh?" said one of the mates. "What ye be doin' here, boy?"

"Aw, just throw him overboard," growled another, and Manjiro recognized the sailor who had stared at him that first night—the one with the cold, blue eyes and yellow curls. The man snatched him by the back of his shirt and dangled him over the side of the boat.

Manjiro felt water seeping into his shoes.

"He'll only be in the way," the man said.

"Avast, Jolly!" It was the captain. "Set him down gently. In the *boat,* if you please." The captain had entered their small boat. He looked at Manjiro.

"You again, is it? Well, we're one man short since young

Thomas took ill, so we'll see what stuff you are made of. You can follow orders, can't you?"

Manjiro nodded. He wasn't completely sure what the captain had asked, but thought it was best to agree with him.

"Take up that oar, then. Jolly, to your oar."

Manjiro sat on a bench and, when the order came, began to row.

"Now, listen to me, all of ye," said the captain, who stood at the stern, holding the tiller. "Your main job is to row, and to row like vengeance. Don't ye be losing your nerve—and no loud noises. Not a hair on your heads may tremble, yet your backs must heave to. Now, pull, me heroes—pull!"

Three other boats had also set off from the ship, each with a six-man crew. They all rowed so hard, Manjiro wondered if they were in a race. But a race to where? Since he faced backward to row, he could not see where they were going. When he glanced over his shoulder, he saw nothing but water. He noticed long, spearlike weapons in the boat, and hoped it wasn't Japanese boys they were going after, like Goemon said.

The captain kept the encouragement going from the stern. Manjiro did like the others and kept his head down and rowed as hard as he could.

Jolly, whose oar was directly behind Manjiro's, hissed at

him. "Yer a heap of trouble, ye filthy, spying Chinaman. . . . Eating our lobscouse, drinkin' our water. Yer nothin' but an ignorant pagan. . . . We'll be setting you off on the first desert island we spy."

"That's where he come from, Jolly," said Edward, a boy a little older than Manjiro who sat on the bench just ahead of him. "That won't frighten him. Anyways, he don't understand a word you're saying."

"That right, you godless cannibal?" Jolly breathed down his neck.

"Jolly!" the captain spoke sharply. "I don't know what you're grumbling about up there—but let's have some hearty rowing, eh? Crack your backbones! Burst your hearts and liver and lungs, me lads. Pull! But merrily, merrily. Plum duff for supper if we get there first!"

Manjiro didn't know what a Chinaman was, or a pagan, or a plum duff, but of them all, he thought he would prefer the plum duff.

"Harpooner, stand by your iron," the captain said, his voice a whisper.

Manjiro heard Jolly abandon the bench and move to the bow of the boat. Why? Manjiro wondered. Stealing a quick glance over his shoulder, he felt his heart rise to his throat.

The water around them seemed to boil, then heave, and

then, up from the sea rose a great black shape. Like a mountain rising out of the sea, a massive head appeared, looming over the boat, its enormous eye staring straight at Manjiro.

"*Kujira!*" Manjiro gasped. Whale. Now he understood. He understood everything. The long, sharp, spearlike things in the boat, the tubs filled with coiled rope, the lookout on the mast—everything made sense. Except, in another way, it didn't make any sense at all.

Jolly stood, poised with the long harpoon, on the bow of the boat. Despite his meanness, Manjiro had to admire him, ready to hurl what looked like a pine needle at that great, hulking creature. There was something magnificent in his bravery and the courage of all these men, who rowed their tiny boat up to and not away from such a monster—more dangerous than a dragon.

The beast's damp breath washed over them, and the captain yelled, "Give it to him!"

The harpoon was thrown; the line hissed as it played out. There was a moment when Manjiro wished he could reach out and pluck it back. The whale was magnificent, too. A beautiful, glistening creature! Such a big amount of life to take!

Manjiro turned back to his oar. He heard the sound of the harpoon plunging into the whale's flesh. Then a second one.

"Stern all!" the captain cried and all hands heaved at the oars, rowing in reverse as hard as they could.

The whale lashed out in pain, its tail striking the sea with a sound like thunder. One blow would reduce their boat to splinters and send them all to the bottom of the sea. Manjiro hoped they could row far, far away from the whale. But the harpoon embedded in its back was attached to a line that was attached to the boat.

Suddenly, the little boat lurched forward. The whale plunged ahead and then struck off swimming, towing them behind so fast it felt as if a gale were blowing.

"Nantucket sleigh ride!" one of the mates hollered. The boat flew along the surface, leaping from crest to crest of the waves with a *bang! bang! bang!* The mates whooped or prayed or clung to the boat with all their might.

Manjiro had not imagined that he could ever experience anything faster or more frightening than when their fishing boat had skimmed down the sides of the giant waves in the storm. But now he knew he had never flown so fast as in this small boat being towed by this enormous beast. Surely, he thought, they would travel from one end of the ocean to the other.

The spray flying over the side thoroughly drenched them

and made it impossible to see—or even breathe. Manjiro realized he had not taken a breath for what seemed like long minutes. He glanced at Edward, who was hunched over and shaking, his knuckles white as they gripped the gunnels of the boat. Manjiro reached out to touch him, then noticed the water sloshing on the bottom of the boat, covering his boots.

A bucket floated in the briny water and he snagged it and started bailing.

"There's me brave lad," the captain cried. "That's thinking!"

Manjiro hadn't been thinking at all. During the big storm, he had spent long days scooping the water out of their little fishing boat. It had become instinctive.

The line attached to the harpoon whistled out of the tubs.

The other end of the line, which had been wrapped around a post in the stern, was smoking from the friction.

"Water on the loggerhead!" the captain yelled.

Manjiro tossed the water from the bucket onto the smoking line.

"Lad," the captain said, "you were born for this work!"

Suddenly the whale burst out of the water in an explosion of foam. It thrashed with its great tail, coming near to knocking the boat over two or three times. Then it swam around and around in smaller and smaller circles, beat the water with its tail, gave a tremendous shudder, and rolled on its side. At that moment, Jolly plunged a long iron lance into its lungs; the whale's spray gushed red, and it lay still at last.

In the deep quiet that followed, Manjiro realized he was shaking. His teeth clattered together. He was wet, cold, and perhaps more afraid than he'd ever been. He felt exhilarated, disgusted, thrilled, giddy with excitement, repulsed, and deeply sad. All these feelings washed over him in nauseating waves.

As a Buddhist, Manjiro had learned that it was wrong to kill—not just people, but living creatures. Of course, Manjiro had killed plenty of fish. In a country like his, surrounded by water and filled with people who needed to eat, it was natural to eat fish. In some villages, whales were sometimes caught. But even a small fish deserved a prayer of gratitude. The fishermen he knew never took fish without remembering to leave grateful offerings at shrines for such purposes.

And this—this was such an enormous being—much more than a big fish. Something with a large spirit! He felt they should say a prayer asking forgiveness for what they had done and express gratitude to the whale for the gift of its life.

Instead, one of his boat mates leaped out and stood on the creature's back. Then, without ceremony, he cut a hole in the whale's head and pulled a rope through it.

• • •

For hours they rowed, towing the heavy corpse back to the ship. As the sun set and darkness descended, Manjiro began to gnaw on a problem: What were they planning to *do* with this whale? Were they going to cook up all the whale meat in those big ovens on the deck? There was no way the few men on board could eat so much meat or transport it any distance before it would spoil.

While Manjiro puzzled over this, Jolly mumbled under his breath, ". . . little heathen . . . wretched pagan . . . dirty, spying Chinaman . . ." over and over, with the rhythm of the oars.

Manjiro, exhausted from the day's events, tried to concentrate on the oars' words: *splash . . . whoosh . . . splash . . . click . . . splash . . .*

As the wind died, the others began to sort Jolly's voice from the creaking, clicking, and splashing.

"Jolly," said one of the mates, "we've tired of your name-calling—and for what? He's just a boy. He's not done anything wrong."

"Can't you at least call him by his name? He *has* a name, hasn't he?"

"Boy, what's your name? Name?"

"Name," Manjiro repeated wearily. He could no longer concentrate to speak the strange language.

"He's simple-minded."

"Even if he is, doesn't mean he can't have a name."

"He has a name," Edward said. "It's Mung something, I think."

"Mung? What kind of name is that? He should have a proper name, like John."

"That's enough from all of ye," the captain interrupted. "Henceforth, I expect this boy to be treated with respect. He has proved himself today as steady and quick-thinking as any of ye, if not more so. Jolly, I don't want to ever hear such foul talk from you again."

Manjiro realized the captain was scolding Jolly. Although he was relieved the name-calling was over for the time being, he knew that now Jolly would hate him more than ever. Manjiro shivered with the memory of being dangled over the side of the boat. He hoped he never ran into Jolly alone on deck in the dark night. He knew he was still skinny enough that he could be slipped into the water with hardly a splash.

"Henceforth," the captain said, "I want ye to call this boy by his new whaling name: John Mung."

"Hear, hear!" the men cheered. All except Jolly, whom Manjiro could feel scowling behind him.

And so, as the moon rose, laying a pale ribbon of light across the whale's back, Manjiro became John Mung, whale hunter.

5

OIL

After all the whaleboats returned to the ship, lamps were lit and the work of butchering began.

Manjiro leaned over the bulwark to watch three men who stood on a platform suspended above the water. Beneath them, sharks tore great chunks of flesh from the whale. The men on the cutting platform jabbed at them occasionally with their spades while they worked at stripping from the whale the thick layer of outer fat called blubber. The huge slabs of thick blubber were winched onto the deck and lowered into the hold.

Drawing by John Mung of a whale to be butchered

"Five and forty more!" came the call from the hands on deck.

"Five and forty more!" The cry was returned from the mates in the hold.

"Five and forty more . . . what?" Manjiro wondered aloud.

"Barrels, John Mung!" Edward said, struggling by with a basket filled with chunks of blubber.

John Mung! So they would really call him that? Now he had not just one, but *two* new names—two names like a samurai would have. But barbarian names. Manjiro shuddered a little.

"See these, John Mung?" Edward held up a chunk of blubber that had been cut so that its slices fanned out like the pages of a book. "Bible leaves. Into the tryworks they go!" he said, tossing the chunk into one of the giant pots on the deck—the ones Goemon had said were to cook Japanese boys.

Manjiro tried to repeat "bible leaves." More impossible English words.

"See that?" Edward pointed into the bubbling pot. "Oil, Mung." Then he called out, "Oil!"

And the crew sang, "Five and forty more!"

Manjiro puzzled over this as he stood in the swirl of men and the clouds of stinking black smoke.

Another basket of whale chunks was carried past, and

Manjiro slid out of the way. Already the deck was slick with blood and greasy soot. Soon he, too, was covered with soot, oil, and blood, and was so tired he had to lean against a mast to stay standing. And yet he couldn't imagine sleeping. There was so much to see and think about. His head spun with questions.

"Go to bed, Mung," said Mr. Aken, the man everyone called Itch. "Look at you—you'd fall down if the mainmast wasn't proppin' you up."

"I learn!" Manjiro said.

"You can't learn it all at once," Itch said.

Manjiro pointed to his head. "Many pockets!" he said. Soon, when he was home in Japan, he would go to these "pockets" and pull out this new knowledge he had stored away.

Itch laughed and shook his head. "There'll be more of the same tomorrow," he said, returning to his tasks.

Manjiro saw Denzo and watched him as if from across an ocean of time. Was it only this morning that he had last spoken with him? It seemed like days or weeks had passed. He crossed the deck to speak to him.

"What happened to you?" Denzo said. "Goemon said he saw you rowing one of the boats."

"Yes," Manjiro said. "I was."

"You were part of this . . . this . . . ," Denzo turned to

gesture to the scene and stopped talking to watch as a bizarre occurence unfolded before them.

The whale's gigantic head was swinging above the deck, having been hoisted out of the water on thick ropes. As soon as it was lowered to the deck, several mates worked to slice open its forehead. Denzo and Manjiro gasped as two men stepped right inside it, and exclaimed as they began scooping out a yellowish goo, which hardened to a pearly white wax while Denzo and Manjiro watched. This waxy substance went into a special cask and was carried belowdecks.

"What do you suppose they do with all this oil and . . . whatever that stuff is?" Manjiro asked Denzo.

Denzo shook his head. "If you doubted they were barbarians, this"—he gestured to the roiling black smoke, the blood and grease on the deck, the sharks seething in the water around the ship— "this should convince you."

"Our countrymen kill whales, too," Manjiro said.

"Yes," Denzo said. "But not like this. You know how they do it—at home, whole villages work together to capture a whale in a net to drown it. Then they tow the creature to shore, butcher it, and distribute the meat to many people. They use all the parts—all the meat, all the bones, everything. But this—this is barbaric. Look at this waste!" Denzo nodded toward the men who shoved the carcass away from the ship, with most of the meat still intact. The sharks attacked it with such frenzy that the water seemed to boil around it.

"All that meat! Gone to waste!" Denzo said and shuddered. "They must be very stupid to throw away the best part. Stupid and cruel. Perhaps if they run out of food, they will do that to us!"

Manjiro's stomach clenched. Was that true? After today, anything seemed possible. He had participated in their barbaric ritual. They had given him a name like theirs. Did that make him a barbarian, too?

For days, the work went on. After the blubber had been boiled into oil, the oil packed into barrels, and the barrels stored belowdecks, and when the stinking black smoke had ceased rising into the air—even after all that, the work was still not done.

For then the scrubbing began. The soot, oil, and blood had to be scrubbed out of the wooden decking. By this time, Manjiro was tired of watching. He wanted to *do* something, and he thought he was not so stupid that he couldn't scrub a deck. He was just about to offer to help, when a voice spoke to him in Japanese.

He turned to see Denzo and Goemon staring at him.

"What do you think you're doing?" Denzo said.

"Denzo-san!" Manjiro said. "I . . . I thought I would help."

"No. That would not be appropriate." Denzo motioned to Manjiro to walk with them along the deck, out of the way. "Manjiro-chan," he said softly, "I feel it is important for me, as the leader of our group, to watch out for you. Now, listen to me. It is better for you to stay away, so that you don't become tainted by their ways. They are corrupting you. Already you walk with their swagger. You are forgetting your manners and addressing all of us as your equals. You neglect to bow. Just now—you did not acknowledge me. You don't even bow to the captain of this ship!"

"He asked me not to."

"You see!" Goemon said. "He is trying to corrupt you. He is making you turn away from all that is right and good. You are being poisoned, Manjiro-chan, just as I warned."

Manjiro thought, If I'm eating poison, I might as well lick the plate, but he didn't say it. There was no reason to be rude. Instead, he bowed to Denzo and said, "Thank you for reminding me of things I should not forget."

Was he being corrupted without realizing it? Manjiro wondered later, sitting on his bunk in the forecastle. He jammed his hands in his trouser pockets and felt the hardtack he had tucked away there this morning. It had been forgotten in the excitement.

He reached under the bunk for the box where he kept such bits of food. When he pulled it out, the lid flapped open—the box was empty!

6

DISAPPOINTMENT

A deep belch issued forth from the gloom, and Manjiro squinted at the shadows. There was Jolly, picking his teeth with a small sliver of baleen.

"You!" Manjiro said, forgetting his fear of the burly man. "I save that food for my family."

"There's no point to that," Jolly snarled, the toothpick still clenched between his teeth. "Ye'll be whistling up a wind if ye think ye'll ever see yer family again."

Manjiro held Jolly's gaze. Was he lying? Or did he know something Manjiro didn't?

Jolly sneered. "Cap'n won't take you back to yer godforsaken country. Savages and beasts that they are, they'd boil us in big pots and skin us, too. They'd do the same to you. That's how you can tell they're no better than animals." Jolly shoved his face up close to Manjiro. "Ye won't be going home again," he said. Tiny crumbs of hardtack trembled in his mustache.

Manjiro felt like the empty box, swept clean of every crumb. It wasn't his stomach that was empty, though; it was his heart. These people were not his friends. They were not his people. Denzo was right. He should avoid them and their cruel ways.

He set the box under his bed and went above decks to stand at the bulwark. He strained his eyes, hoping to make out something like the shape of his homeland. But the sea was large, bigger than he'd ever imagined. And now he realized that the sparkling path of light that often glittered on the water, and which he had always imagined was leading them toward home, was actually leading them *away*.

"Boy!"

Manjiro turned to see the captain squinting down at him.

"I am told you are learning English quickly. Is that true?"

Manjiro bowed.

"Does that mean yes? All this blasted bowing! Stand up and say 'aye' if that's what you mean."

Manjiro stood up and said, "Aye."

"And look me in the eye when you say that."

Manjiro forced himself to look—quickly—into the captain's eyes.

The captain had a habit of squeezing one of his eyes shut and regarding a person with the other one. He could, Manjiro thought, communicate more with that one eye than most people would be able to with three. It took only one dark, piercing eye to convey his many moods—as many moods as the sea. This time, though, Manjiro didn't know what to make of his gaze, and he didn't want to know, either.

"Good," the captain said. "I want to explain something to you, so you can explain to your friends."

Manjiro crammed his hands in his pockets and fidgeted. Denzo was the leader of their group, and he should be the one who spoke to the captain. But Denzo, like the others, didn't want anything to do with the barbarians, including learning their language, so it had fallen to Manjiro to interpret what the others said.

"Come and have a cup of tea in my quarters," the captain said.

Manjiro did not see that he had any choice, and he followed, his brow tight with anger. He tried to let go of it. A samurai should not feel anger toward his enemy, he remembered his father telling him. A courteous samurai, his father said, would wash his hair before battle so if his head was taken it would smell sweet for his enemy.

Manjiro snorted to think of it. These barbarians and their ship stunk so badly, he doubted that a head of washed hair could be appreciated through the stench.

"Pardon?" the captain said, reacting to Manjiro's snort.

Manjiro ducked his head and said nothing.

They arrived at the captain's quarters, by far the most

elegant on the ship. The captain gestured to a chair, and Manjiro sat down. He would never get used to sitting this way, he thought, and why should he? Only an ignorant foreigner would sit like this. He should show them the correct way to sit—back on your heels, or cross-legged on the floor. But perhaps these strangers were incapable of sitting that way. They weren't as supple or as graceful as Manjiro's countrymen.

A teapot rattling on a tray announced the cook's entrance. Captain Whitfield poured the strong, black tea into two cups. In another cup there were some sweet grains like sand, called "sugar." Manjiro wondered how he might save some of these grains for his little sisters. But then he remembered he was not going home, and the sweet tea turned bitter in his mouth.

"You have learned English quickly," the captain said. "I want to explain something to you and I want you to tell this to Denzo and the others."

Manjiro took a great gulp of tea. This was a big responsibility. It was important that he understand!

"The day we found you, I had sent men to look for turtles near your island. We didn't know you were there, but when the men saw you, they knew you must be fed—or die."

Manjiro nodded. That was true.

The captain continued, "So they brought you back to

the *John Howland* and I agreed to take you aboard, with the intention of bringing you back to your homeland, if that were possible. But I suspect you may be from Japan. If that is so, your country does not treat foreign visitors kindly. Once a ship named the *Morrison* tried to enter Edo Bay in order to return some shipwrecked sailors like yourselves, but before they could even explain the reason for their visit, they were fired upon—repeatedly—and were forced to retreat.

"I can't afford to lose the *John Howland* or jeopardize the lives of my men," the captain said. "Stories are told of how even your countrymen, once they have gone beyond their shores, are not allowed to return. They say they are imprisoned, tortured, even executed! I will not send you home, only for you to die! Do you understand now why we cannot take you home?"

Manjiro nodded, biting back tears.

Then Captain Whitfield asked Manjiro to tell about his family.

"I have three sister and one brother. I have mother, no father. My one brother older but he weak. I take care family." He stared down at his teacup, tears trembling in his eyes. Of course, he was *not* taking care of his family.

"Ah," the captain said. "You were the breadwinner for the family."

"Breadwin?" Manjiro looked up.

"You brought food to the family."

"I try, but no good," Manjiro said. He hung his head again.

"It must be very hard for you to be so far away," the captain said. "You miss your family. Your family must miss you very much, too. Can you tell me about your homeland?"

Manjiro stared into his teacup. He longed to describe the green, rounded hills that rose from the jagged rocks and cliffs of the coast. He wanted to tell about the steamy summer days when the only sounds were the waves rushing up on the beach and the shrill cry of the kite or the warbler's curious song. If only he could explain how he loved to walk the narrow lane that led to his family's hut when it was dappled with sunlight or shining with rain, how friendly was the creak of the door when it opened and the gentle thud it made when it shut. How cool and pleasant it was inside, with his mother sewing or cooking and his brother and sisters playing happily beside her. How could he tell the captain he had run away from this, and how deeply he regretted it?

He did not have the words.

Yet when Manjiro finally looked up, Captain Whitfield's eyes showed he had understood the longing Manjiro felt.

"Someday, son, I hope you will be able to go home. I am sorry it cannot be soon," he said. The captain picked up a funny-looking musical instrument. A violin, he called it, then played something on it that Manjiro realized must be music. It was a strange sound, a little sad.

As he listened, Manjiro's eyes drifted around the room, taking in the many unusual objects, finally resting on an open book on the captain's desk. Maybe the captain even knew how to read!

As if understanding his thought, Captain Whitfield picked up the book and began to read aloud.

Manjiro had a hard time following, but he was sure it was a poem. It had a "shipwrecked brother" in it who saw footprints and got up and started doing something. The gist of the poem, he thought, was that we should do the best we can with whatever fate the gods give us in our lives, and perhaps we can inspire others who come after us.

Manjiro stared at the captain. He had never imagined that a barbarian could appreciate poetry. Or play music. Or express kindness.

Then he realized his mouth was hanging open, and he quickly shut it and ducked his head. His eye stopped at a small portrait of a woman on the desk.

"That is—was—my wife," Captain Whitfield said quietly. "She passed away before we shipped out."

"You have childrens?" Manjiro asked.

The captain shook his head, coughed, and said, "No." He paused. "No," he said again.

"You have no childrens; I have no father." Manjiro said, and their eyes met for a moment.

When Manjiro left the room soon after, he tried to identify what he was feeling. He was no longer afraid. He was no longer angry. He was, perhaps, a little amazed. A little surprised. And maybe even a little bit happy.

7

SHIP LIFE

As the days went on, Manjiro learned how to shorten sail, sheet home, trice up, and trim and make sail. He learned how to scrub the deck with soft sandstone tools known as "holy stones." The main deck was scrubbed with a "bible" and the hard-to-reach corners with a "prayer book."

"They aren't really those things," Itch said. "A bible is a holy book, see, and a prayer book is, too. You wouldn't *really* scrub a deck with them."

Manjiro spent the day puzzling over that and over all the words he'd learned that had more than one meaning: The *bow* was the front of the vessel. But it was also what he did when he bent from the waist when meeting someone. The fins on a whale's tail were called its *fluke*. But a *fluke* also meant a stroke of luck—like the fact that Captain Whitfield had sent a boat to fetch turtles on Bird Island that day. That was a stroke of luck—a fluke. Or was it fruke? R's and L's were impossible. What was the difference between *grass* and *glass*, for instance?

Aye, I, and *eye*. *See, sea,* and C. *Weigh, way,* and *whey*.

Would he ever be able to learn this strange language?

As his English improved, and as he became more useful around the *John Howland,* it was easier for him to get to know the crew. He made friends with many of them, including the men who had rescued them from the island. They had all seemed so big and so hairy and so fierce when he'd first encountered them, but now he knew them as mostly kind and pleasant men. He had ceased to identify them by their skin or hair colors; now he knew them by their names and personalities. He knew that Edward was learning to play the pennywhistle, and Parden made beautiful scrimshaw pictures. Mr. Q. was big but gentle, and Josiah really liked to eat. Biscuit was an old salt who always knew the juiciest bits of gossip. Isaiah, one of the men who was so very black, always seemed to have something funny to say—though Manjiro didn't often get the jokes, the others laughed. Francis was the quickest up the rigging and taught Manjiro how to climb the ratlines to the crosstrees. These men came from countries all over the world, but most of them came from a place called America.

"What is 'America'?" Manjiro asked as he worked at scrubbing around the tryworks.

"Vast heaving!" Edward exclaimed. "But have you never heard of America?"

Manjiro shook his head, and the deckhands put down

their "bibles" and "prayer books" to gather around the boy who had never heard of America.

"Where did you come from? Did you live your whole life on that bare rock from which we plucked you?"

"Oh! I'll bet he's from that country that locks us out and their countrymen in," said Francis.

"'Tis sealed and shuttered," said Parden.

"Many's the whaler that could have used its ports to make repairs or take on fresh food and water, but never a soul can tread the shores of Japan," said Mr. Q., tossing a scrubbing stone from hand to hand.

"I've heard tell they put shipwrecked sailors in tiny cages," Edward said, "afore they kill 'em!"

"They're godless cannibals," Jolly grumbled from his post. He hadn't bothered to gather with the others, but he was listening just the same, Manjiro noticed.

"No need to take it out on the boy," Biscuit said. "'Tisn't his fault."

"They're all alike, them people," Jolly growled. "You can't take the savage out of savages."

"But how is it you never learned about America?" Edward asked.

Relieved at the change of subject, Manjiro said, "We never heard of it. What is it?"

"Why, she's only the greatest nation on earth, isn't she? She has the finest vessels, the smartest captains, the strongest men, and . . ." Francis winked at Manjiro, "the prettiest young ladies in all the world."

"That's not what you told that raven-haired maid on the Canary Islands," Biscuit said.

"She was an exception," said Francis.

The others laughed.

"Boy," Parden said, "if ye think buttons and pockets are a wonder, then yer eyes would pop and yer mind swim if ye beheld the wonders of America."

"Will we ever go there?" Manjiro said.

"Will we go there?" Itch laughed. "Who do you think we're collecting all this whale oil *for*? Why, it's for our own dear kin, to light their lamps, to oil their machines, and to supply a hundred fine things with all the parts the whale provides, such as—" Itch broke off and the other men were suddenly silent. Captain Whitfield stood over them, squinting down at them with one blazing eye. As one, they leaped back to their work.

Later that evening, Manjiro found Captain Whitfield standing at the taffrail gazing out at the silver-tipped waves.

"You are come from America, too?" Manjiro asked.

"Yes, indeed!" Captain Whitfield said.

"It is land of wonders," Manjiro said. "The mates tell me."

"Ah," said the captain. "So it is. They call it the land of opportunity."

"What is opportunity?"

"It means . . . possibility. It means, with hard work and discipline, a man with hopes and dreams can see them come to fruition. I wonder . . ." Captain Whitfield paused for a moment and then went on. "What are *your* hopes and dreams?"

"Hopes and dreams?" Manjiro said.

"What do you hope to do with your life—who do you hope to become?"

Manjiro had never thought of such things. He had always known what work he would do. Of course, he would have liked to bring honor to his family, and he remembered how he'd once said he wanted to be a samurai. But that was not a real dream, because it could never happen. Now . . . well, now he didn't know.

"Future is like ocean," he said. "Big mystery, many danger, much beautiful. It full of . . ." He didn't know the word to describe what he was thinking, so he just stretched his arms wide.

"Opportunity?" Captain Whitfield said.

Manjiro nodded. "Yes," he said. "Opportunity."

8

THE INVITATION

December 1841, Oahu, Sandwich Islands

The day started off like any ordinary day. Manjiro was sitting on the foredeck trying to untangle a line while Itch read to him from the *Polynesian,* Honolulu's newspaper. "Arrived: November 20, 1841. *John Howland,* New Bedford, twenty-four months, fourteen hundred barrels," he read.

"What does it mean?" Manjiro asked.

Drawing of Oahu with ships in the harbor

"Ah, well. It means this here vessel, the *John Howland,* having sailed from New Bedford, Massachusetts, arrived in Honolulu after twenty-four months at sea—six months with you aboard—carrying fourteen hundred barrels of spermaceti whale oil. Nineteen whales already. A fine start, isn't it?" he said merrily.

Manjiro knew that the ship would sail for perhaps another year or more before heading for home.

"D'ye fancy the sailing life?" Itch said.

Manjiro looked up. How could he explain how his heart lifted when the sails unfurled? How the sails seemed to him like great wings with which he could fly across the ocean?

"You were lucky to have been rescued by this captain," Itch said. "Not every captain is as fair-minded and generous. There's some who would have made slaves out of you, I warrant. But not Whitfield. He's an honest and fair-minded man, pious and plainspoken. There be no drink aboard his vessel, and there be no whale chasing on Sundays, neither. And no flogging. He's no hypocrite, like some whose names I could mention. They claim to be godly men, yet treat their crew like dogs. Some ship owners provision their vessels so poorly that a poor sailor can barely keep flesh on his bones."

Manjiro was happy to hear Itch say what he believed to be true—that Captain Whitfield was a good man. He wanted to ask Itch all kinds of questions about the captain, but he stopped when he saw Denzo and the others hurrying toward him.

"We have good news!" Denzo said. "The captain has found new homes for us on this island!"

Manjiro swallowed hard.

"Aren't you happy?" Goemon said. Goemon must be relieved to be done with sailing, Manjiro thought, and he nodded.

"We might have a chance to try to go home, too!" Jusuke continued. "Ships from here sometimes sail close to Japan, we have heard."

"But there is something else," Denzo said, then cleared his throat solemnly. "I have had a conversation with Captain Whitfield"—in the previous weeks, Denzo had finally picked up enough English to communicate a little with the captain—"about you."

Oh, oh, Manjiro thought, I'm in trouble. He looked down at the knotted line in his lap—line he, himself, had tangled. He made many mistakes. He remembered that just the other day he had dropped a bucket overboard. It had floated for a few moments before sinking to the bottom of the harbor. He was sure to be punished.

"Captain Whitfield has asked me if I would allow you to

travel with him to America, to live with him as his son," Denzo said.

Manjiro's heart leaped. The captain's son! "What did you say?" were the first words from his mouth. Then, remembering his manners, he bowed and said, "Excuse me, Denzo-san. That is to say, might I beg to know what you answered?"

"I do not feel it is right to split up our group," Denzo said. "We have suffered much together. And, as the leader of this group, I am responsible for your safety and well-being. How would it look if we were to return to Japan—without you?"

Manjiro bowed his head. He hadn't thought of these things.

"On the other hand . . . ," Denzo said, and paused. Manjiro held his breath. "The captain has been so good to us, I do not feel that I can refuse him." Manjiro looked up and waited. "I told the captain the decision is up to you."

Manjiro opened his mouth to speak, but no words came out. Thoughts collided in his mind. To see America . . . but to possibly miss a chance to return home to his mother and his family. To learn a thousand new things . . . but to go to a strange place where people might hate and reject him. To feel again the lift of his heart when the sails filled with wind and the ship seemed to soar over the ocean . . . but to have to say good-bye to his comrades with whom he'd shared so much . . .

"Denzo-san." Manjiro bowed and stammered. "I . . . uh . . . I . . . don't know what to do!"

"You do not have to make your decision right away," Denzo said. "The *John Howland* does not sail for several days."

Jusuke winked at him. "Perhaps you should take advice of your pillow."

It was the same saying in English almost, Manjiro realized. Once, his friend Itch had told him to "sleep on it" when he'd had a decision to make.

Americans might not be so *terribly* different from us, he thought. "Yes. I will take the advice of my pillow," Manjiro said. "I will sleep on it."

But he could hardly sleep. Manjiro spent the next few days trying to make the right decision. One afternoon he walked on the beach with Goemon. While he picked up pretty shells—shells he hoped someday to give his mother—he thought about his choice. He looked at the indentations his feet had made on the beach and thought of the captain's poem.

"Goemon," he said, "maybe one day we will leave footprints in the sands of time."

"What are you talking about?" Goemon said.

"There's a poem Captain Whitfield is teaching me. It's by a person called Long Fellow. I think that means he is very tall.

The poem goes like this:

"Lives of great men all remind us
We can make our lives sublime
And, departing, leave behind us
Footprints on the sands of time.

"Then there are some other verses, but I don't remember how they go. It has 'forlorn and shipwrecked brothers' in it, though, and more footprints. The last verse goes:

"Let us, then, be up and doing
With a heart for any fate
Something . . . something . . . something . . . something . . .
Learn to labor and to wait."

"What's that supposed to mean?" Goemon said, kicking at a stone.

"I think it means that we can do great things in our lives—things people will remember."

"No, we can't!" Goemon said. "We are just humble fishermen. Only big important people—the shogun, the daimyo, maybe this captain—*they* can do great things."

"That's what I used to think, too. Back home, I always knew that I would just be a fisherman. I never questioned it; I know we never asked ourselves what—or who—we wanted to become. Why should we? We always knew. But what if we could do important things, too? Captain Whitfield said that if I work very hard, someday I could become a captain of a ship!"

"That's as stupid as when you said you were going to become a samurai!" Goemon said. "You shouldn't want to be what you can't be."

"Captain Whitfield said any smart, ambitious person can become a captain."

"Not you."

"Why not me? Captain Whitfield says he personally knows a former slave who is the captain of a whaling ship now."

"Captain Whitfield says this, Captain Whitfield says that. You listen to everything he says. He makes you think wrong thoughts. You listen to the foreigners; you believe them. You're like *them*," Goemon cried, his voice breaking. "I don't know you anymore!"

Manjiro wondered if that was so. Had he changed? Perhaps it would be better to remain with Denzo and the others and stay in his rightful place. But if he sailed with the captain, he would have the chance to learn many things, to see the world, and to have, at last, a father.

But then he thought of his mother and how worried she must be. Perhaps she thought he was dead. Had she heard what had happened to him? Maybe she thought he had run away with no intention of ever returning! If only he had told his mother where he was going—and that he planned to return! Perhaps it would be best to try to get back to his family as fast as possible.

Then he thought of the times he'd spent with Captain Whitfield, asking question after question in his halting English, the captain patiently answering every one. The day they had sailed into this harbor, they had stood together early in the morning, breathing in the fragrance of the island before watching it emerge out of the mist. Manjiro told the captain how two gods, Izanami and Izanagi, had created an island—his home—out of sweet-smelling mist and fog. Something like that was happening with their friendship, he thought. It was like a tranquil island in a stormy sea.

9

SEVEN BREATHS

Two days before the *John Howland* was to leave Honolulu, Manjiro still hadn't made a decision. Then, Captain Whitfield told Manjiro that he and the others had an "invitation."

"I have invitation?" Manjiro said. "Is that bad?"

Captain Whitfield chuckled. "No, not usually. An invitation is when someone *invites* you to come and visit. In this case, an acquaintance of mine, Dr. Gerritt Judd, wants to meet you and your friends. He has some coins and small items he wonders if you can identify."

The next day, at Dr. Judd's home, the fishermen examined the coins and a smoking pipe.

"But where do you come by these things?" Manjiro asked their host.

Dr. Judd told them about some other shipwrecked sailors. The captain and a couple of crew members had died, but the others had been rescued and made their way to Honolulu, like Manjiro and his friends.

Manjiro thought of the graves on Bird Island. "Where are they now?" he asked.

"They have tried to go back to Japan by way of China," Dr. Judd said. "We don't know how they fared. But tell us, are you from the same country?"

"Yes! Yes!" The fishermen nodded.

The captain unrolled a large scroll of paper. The five friends stared down at it.

"What is . . . ?" Manjiro said.

"Why, it's a chart!" Captain Whitfield said. "A map! Look here. It's a picture that shows the world."

The fishermen wondered over the strangeness of it, while Manjiro translated the captain's words.

"This is where we are." Captain Whitfield pointed to a little necklace of green spots on an ocean of blue. "These are the Sandwich Islands, governed by King Kamehameha. Since he is friendly with the United States, there are now many Americans here, doing business and serving as missionaries and doctors."

Captain Whitfield pointed to the small island where the fishermen had been found, and then to another group of islands that lay to the northwest of that island. "Your home," he said.

"No!" The fishermen shook their heads.

"Our country is much, much bigger than that!" Denzo said.

Captain Whitfield smiled. "Perhaps since your country does not allow anyone in or out, they do not know the true size or shape of the world—even of their own country."

Manjiro did not translate that for the others, fearing it might anger them.

Behind him, his friends whispered to one another in Japanese.

"What crazy ideas they have!" Toraemon said.

The others agreed that their country could not be so insignificant.

Manjiro said, "Just because it is small, that doesn't mean it is insignificant." He wanted to add, "Surely you have seen enough ocean by now to understand that the world is bigger than you could have imagined. Surely you must realize that these whaling men, who have sailed to all its corners, must know more of the world than our countrymen—who never go anywhere!" But he bit his tongue. He did not want to offend them, and he knew they still clung to the ideas they had learned at home, that their country was best and biggest and all others were filled with barbarians.

It was true the Americans were somewhat uncivilized. They were loud and dirty and let their hair grow in unruly knots and tangles. They swore and cussed and spat. They often ate with their hands, and rather like animals. They didn't smell too good! And their whaling practice was a very bloody business indeed.

But they knew a lot of things about which Manjiro knew nothing, and the thing they knew the most was the thing he knew the least: the size and shape and scope of the world. How could you not want to understand the world in which you lived?

His friends had turned away from the map, but Manjiro continued to stare at it, marveling at the many places and countries about which he knew nothing. His heart pounded as if his chest were a hollow drum. Look at this world! So vast! So wide! Huge masses of land spread across it; multitudes of green and brown islands dotted the blue expanse of the oceans. He felt like a bird contemplating the sky.

He turned to see Captain Whitfield standing over him. "That," the captain said, pointing to a large landmass on the map, "is America. This is the United States." He pointed to a small spot on the northeast coast of the United States and said, "*This* is Fairhaven, Massachusetts, where I live."

"The chart is like . . . invitation," Manjiro said, staring at the unfamiliar letters that he knew formed words. "I cannot read the words, but I imagine they say, 'Come and see!'"

The captain patted him on the back. "That isn't what the

words *say*," he said, "but I think that is always what a chart *means*. When I see a place on a chart where I haven't been, I wonder, 'What is that place like?' I look at that place again and again, wondering if something more might be revealed. But there's nothing to be done but to go and see it for myself."

Manjiro nodded, staring at the spot on the map Captain Whitfield said was his home in America.

"In the words of the ancients," his mother had told him, "one should make one's decisions within the space of seven breaths."

Manjiro took seven deep, long breaths. By the last breath, he had made his decision: He would go to America and see it for himself.

10

DANGER!

The captain gave each of the five fishermen a new jacket, a new pair of trousers, and a new overcoat. They were also each presented with five half-dollars to help them get a start in their new lives on the island. Manjiro's eyes grew big as the coins were pressed into his hands. So much money! The only time he'd ever held money like this was when Itch had taught him a magic trick with coins.

Finally, the captain told them the *John Howland* would set sail the next morning.

"I hope I will see you aboard, my lad," he said to Manjiro. "You are a bright boy, bursting with questions." The sadness Manjiro had once seen in his eyes had melted away.

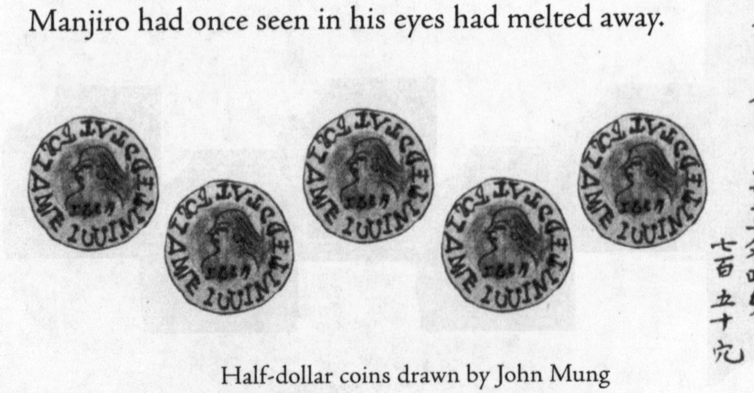

Half-dollar coins drawn by John Mung

Manjiro felt tears spring to his eyes. He wanted to tell Captain Whitfield, "Yes! Yes, I will come along," but he did not. He simply hung his head and murmured his thanks. First, he must try to explain his decision to Goemon.

He and Goemon tried on their new jackets and tucked the paper-wrapped packages of trousers and overcoats under their arms.

"Come down to the beach with me?" he asked Goemon as they stepped out of the house into the silken dusk.

At first the boys jingled the coins in their pockets and chattered about their fine new clothes. Goemon said the money would help them get a start on the island. They would be able to buy seeds for planting and maybe get some chickens, too. But soon they fell into silence as they walked, each immersed in his own thoughts.

Through the trees and far down the beach, Manjiro could hear the native people singing. *Mele* and *hula,* their music and dancing was called. They weren't supposed to do it; the missionaries said it was wrong. Manjiro thought the music was lovely; it had a motion like the sea—it rolled over you and through you like water. Western missionaries had come to Japan, too, a couple of hundred years earlier, and they were one reason Japan had closed its doors to foreigners. Seeing how the native islanders here were expected to change almost everything about their lives for the missionaries, Manjiro could understand why Japan had expelled them.

The boys came to the main street, where music poured from every door. From a church came solemn, stately music and many voices singing together. Out of the doors of taverns came the sounds of pennywhistles and sailors' hearty drinking songs.

So many different voices, here on one island. Manjiro's eyes and ears, all his senses, had been filled with new experiences, new ways of doing things. He had, in fact, found a new way of seeing the world. Not with fear, but with wonder.

"You're not really going to go with those barbarians, are you?" Goemon said, suddenly.

"How can you still call them barbarians," Manjiro said, "after all they've done for us?"

"How can I call them barbarians?" Goemon said. "The food is terrible; the sleeping quarters are cramped and smelly. They stink like pigs. They hardly ever bathe. All that whaling with the choking black smoke and filth and grease! These whaling men are cruel. You can see for yourself how cruel they are!"

Were the men cruel? Yes, and then again, no. Manjiro

knew how cruel they could be in their whaling moments, and yet he saw another side of them, too. They were good-hearted, generous, and something else, too. He didn't have a name for it, but it seemed so natural, like second nature, for them to be kind to others while expecting nothing in return. Captain Whitfield, for instance. He was the very most important person on the ship, and he managed the *John Howland* with authority, and yet he treated everyone with kindness and respect, no matter what the person's rank.

"There's hardly anything they do that makes sense," Goemon went on, "like the way they eat with those awkward utensils."

"Forks?"

"Yes, whatever they're called."

"If you'd bother to learn English," Manjiro said, "things would go better for you."

"It wouldn't help me to eat with those stupid . . . sticks!"

"We're the ones who eat with sticks," Manjiro said. "What's so smart about that?"

"It's easier! It just makes more sense."

"It's only easier because we're used to it. The same way they're used to eating with forks and knives."

"When they bother to use them!" Goemon said, then pointed to a couple walking in the street. "Look how that woman walks with her arm on that man's arm. Don't they know that they shouldn't touch in public—that's just wrong! And, besides, women should always walk behind men."

"Why should women walk behind men?"

"Why? Because it's the way it should be. You're blind to their faults. You've been seduced by them. They give you two names and suddenly you think you're a samurai! I'll tell you what will happen to you. That captain, he will take you home with him and make you his slave! That's what they do in that country, you know—they have slaves."

Manjiro did not think the captain would make him a slave. He really didn't think so. But he was quiet as he and Goemon walked through the trees toward the beach.

Under the trees it was dark, and the boys felt their way along the path that led to the ocean. Seedpods crackled under their feet; the palms hissed overhead. Except for those soft sounds and the surf pounding in the distance, everything seemed quiet and tranquil.

Manjiro wondered how he was ever going to explain to Goemon why he wanted to go to America. He was so immersed in these thoughts that he didn't notice the shadows growing closer, or the crunching footsteps, or even Goemon tugging at his sleeve.

Then Goemon whispered, "It seems as if the shadows have shadows."

Manjiro stared into the darkness, listening. "Yes, and our footsteps have footsteps," he said.

"Maybe they are *oni*!" Goemon whispered. "Evil demons!"

The shadows had become more real and tangible as Manjiro and Goemon walked, and grew so close that Manjiro could smell them. "They might be *oni*," he said, "but they stink like whaling men."

"Run!" Goemon cried and darted away.

Manjiro started to follow but felt himself snatched by the throat. A big hand, strong as iron, gripped him by the neck.

11

THIEVES AND MURDERERS

In Japan it was considered impolite to breathe on another person. People held their hands in front of their mouths to avoid it. The man breathing down Manjiro's neck made no such effort. Rum, sweat, and whale oil—the stench of a whaling man.

"Haul 'em to the fire," said a voice from the darkness. Manjiro was dragged across the sand and into a circle of firelight. Four or five greasy faces appeared, disappeared, and reappeared in the flickering light. A pair of glimmering spectacles, a gleaming gold hoop, an empty grin of a few silver teeth, and the flash of a knife—the kind whale men used to trim bits of flesh from blubber—glinted in the firelight. Goemon was there, too, pale and shivering.

"Look what fine fellows we have here," said the man with silver teeth, whose every S came out as a whistle. "Wif new suits and something a-singin' in their pockets."

"Never did I know how many heathens there were loose in the world," said a familiar voice, "till I started to ship out on whalers. And never did I think I'd have to abide them on my own vessel!"

Jolly stepped into the light and spat in the sand in front of Manjiro. "Everywhere I go, I see them, naked cannibals."

"They ain't naked," said Gold Hoop. "They be as finely dressed as young gentlemen, they be."

Jolly snatched the jug from him and held it to his mouth. The liquid gurgled onto his already glistening beard. "That's because they *steal* their clothes. They're all thieves and murderers. Like this one," Jolly grabbed Manjiro's ear. "Stealin' food from the *John Howland,* he was. I found it all stashed away neat in a box under his bunk, didn't I?"

"That was my food!" Manjiro cried. "You are the one that st—"

"Now he's stealin' the captain's fine woolen clothing," Jolly interrupted, plucking the paper-wrapped packages from their arms and tossing them on the ground. He breathed down into Manjiro's face. "The captain won't think so kindly on you when he finds you even snitched this!" He pulled on a chain that glinted from his pocket. At the end of the little chain dangled a silver disk.

Manjiro had seen the captain pull this thing out of his pocket on many occasions, flip open the silver cover, and consult it.

"Aye, I see you know it," Jolly sneered. "'Tis the captain's watch."

Manjiro felt anger rise in his throat. "*You* stole it!" he cried, and snatched the watch out of Jolly's hands.

"See?" Jolly said. "Just like a monkey trained to snitch things, that's what he does. Can't hardly help himself. Now give it back."

"It belongs to Captain. Not you. I will give it back, tell that you steal."

"Oh, will *ye* now? But he already knows that *ye* stole it. How does he know that? Because I told him. Now, who is he going to believe? His favorite harpooner, choosed by him to ride in his own whaleboat, and with seventeen years' experience on the high seas? Or an illiterated savage boy, green as seaweed? But I'll strike a bargain with ye. Be good little heathens and hand over the silver I knows is in yer pockets, and I'll keep hush about the watch. Also, it would be best if I never sees yer squinty eyes aboard ship again."

"Avast with yer yammering, Jolly," said Gold Hoop. "Let's get the silver and get out of here."

Goemon's face glowed white in the darkness. Manjiro knew that Goemon was trying to keep his face from betraying emotion, but fear played across it—and hatred.

"No." Manjiro tried to speak firmly, but his voice squeaked a little.

The man with the knife spun around suddenly and pointed it at Goemon's pockets. "We can cut the silver out," he growled.

"No!" Goemon cried. He slowly pulled the coins out of his pocket and handed them to the man.

"Now you," the man said, turning to Manjiro.

Manjiro felt anger rise in his throat and tried to choke it down.

"Turn out yer pockets or *I'll* turn 'em out," the man said.

Manjiro pulled his hands from his pockets and held them out. In the palm of his hands he held one smooth pebble, a bit of hardtack, and two small pink shells. But no coins.

Silver Teeth growled, and despite his many missing teeth, snapped like a dog. "That's a child's trick!" he said, slapping the things out of Manjiro's hands. "We'll have none of it. Turn yer pockets out. Now!"

Manjiro turned the pockets of his trousers inside out. They were empty.

Goemon's eyes flew open, but he quickly smoothed his face into an emotionless mask.

"I thought ye said that one had money, too," the one wearing the gold hoop said, turning to Jolly.

"He does!" Jolly hissed. "Shake him! Shake him like a apple tree!" He lunged, but Manjiro ducked.

Everything became a blur of fists and flashing teeth and glinting knives and sweat-glistening skin. Several different faces flickered by: a shock of red whiskers, a toothless grin, a dark-skinned face, and Jolly's coinlike curls.

Manjiro's legs went—or were kicked—out from under him, and he fell heavily into the sand. His hand knocked against something smooth and solid as a sword handle, and he grabbed it, leaped up, and, using it as a weapon, lunged wildly. But it was on fire! He had pulled a burning piece of driftwood from the bonfire. The flames leaped from the burning stick onto Jolly's rum-soaked beard.

Jolly yowled with pain and ran toward the sea, flames leaping out behind him. With a whoop, his friends chased after him, screaming like gulls following a fishing boat.

The boys wasted no time. They grabbed their packages and set off running, after Manjiro had stopped to pick something out of the sand: a shiny silver disk.

Finally, far down the beach, they dropped into the sand.

"Thank you for saving my life," Goemon panted.

"Oh, I don't think they were going to kill us!" Manjiro said.

"They are barbarians," Goemon spat. "You cannot trust them."

Manjiro didn't say anything.

"Surely you can see now why it would have been foolish to go with them."

"Put out your hand," Manjiro said, and when Goemon did, Manjiro slipped five coins into Goemon's palm.

Goemon exclaimed, "How—? Ah, the trick you learned from the first mate." He smiled. "But no! Those are yours! You keep them."

"I won't need money."

"Why not?"

"What am I going to do with money on board a ship?" Manjiro said. "I'll be a crew member and will earn my lay when the journey ends: one one-hundred-fortieth of the profits!"

"You're really going to go with them, aren't you?" Goemon said. "With that crazy man, that Jolly. He wants to kill you!"

"He was drunk," Manjiro said. "He'll probably forget about it."

"I don't think so!" Goemon said. "They'll never accept you, Manjiro. If they were to come to *our* country, they would be killed! And that's what they will do to *you*. As soon as you set foot in America, *if* you ever get that far, they'll cut your head off and put it on a pole, warning other Japanese people to *stay away*. They're all like that crazy man—that Jolly. They all hate us! You'll see."

"There's always going to be someone like Jolly, anywhere we go," Manjiro said. "At least I *know* this one."

Goemon brushed the sand from his Western-style trousers as if he were smoothing a silk kimono. "Go ahead," he said. "Turn your back on us! Turn your back on me! But you are wrong, Manjiro, and someday you will see that you are wrong. You will find out that, like Jusuke says, 'the nail that sticks up gets hammered down.'"

Manjiro pointed to the sky. "Look," he said. Pink light rimmed the eastern horizon and ran down onto the sea.

"Doesn't it look like the light from another world, spilling through a slightly open door?"

"No," Goemon said. "It looks like the sun is about to rise."

"It's like how I feel about America," Manjiro said. "It's as if I see this little bit of light from an open door. It promises . . . I don't know what! But I want to go through that door and find out what is there."

"You, my friend, are crazy," Goemon sighed. "And late. You'd better hurry if you want to get to the ship before she sails."

Manjiro turned to Goemon and bowed. "Friend," he said, "I won't forget you. We will see each other again. I am sure of it."

12

SAILING AWAY

From his post at the stern rail of the *John Howland*, Manjiro watched as Goemon grew smaller and smaller, shrinking to just a spot of color and then disappearing altogether into the island. At last, even the island itself disappeared.

Once, back in Japan, Manjiro had watched a boy flying a kite. The string snapped and the kite soared off into the blue sky and out across the ocean. The boy cried to see his kite disappear, but Manjiro had felt his imagination soar. What might that kite have seen, if it had eyes? What might it have heard if it had ears? Oh, to be a kite, cut loose from its string, Manjiro had thought.

And now he was just like that kite, sailing away into a sea as vast and blue as the sky. Was it wrong to feel exhilarated and alive? Was he wrong to be happy, sailing even farther away from his ancestors and his family?

The sails snapped taut in the wind, and Manjiro—John Mung, whaler—was flying over the ocean, carried along by the ship's great white wings. He had left everything behind. Even his name.

He took a deep breath of salt air and froze. A flame of fear raced through him. Jolly. He had not yet encountered Jolly.

A gruff voice from behind him made him jump. "You, boy! Up in the rigging with you—tar the netting of the mainstay sail. If I have to speak to you again, your hide will pay!"

Manjiro glanced over his shoulder to see Davis, the first mate, glowering at him.

Not pausing to wonder why Mr. Davis was so unhappy with him, Manjiro scrambled up the rigging and got to work right away. At least up here, he could keep an eye out for Jolly.

But soon, he began to mull on another problem. The *tick tick tick* of the halyards against the spars reminded him of the captain's watch. He wanted to give the watch back to the captain, but he couldn't think of how to do it without appearing to be the thief. How could he explain with his broken English how it had come about that he was in possession of the watch, especially against whatever well-crafted story Jolly had made up? Would the captain punish him? He might be so angry that he would set him off at the next island they came to.

As he was considering all the miserable possibilities, he saw Captain Whitfield striding across the deck with those big, sure steps he took. Manjiro was just wondering if he should run farther up the rigging when he heard the captain's voice calling up to him.

"Is that John Mung up there?" The captain squinted up at him like a one-eyed *Hitotsume-kozo* creature.

"Aye, sir," Manjiro called down to him.

"Glad to have you aboard."

"Glad to be aboard, sir." Manjiro gulped. What should he do? Should he say something now? He opened his mouth, then closed it. He couldn't think of what to say. No doubt there would be a better time.

The captain squinted at him expectantly and finally said, "Well?"

"Well?" Manjiro echoed.

"No questions? You don't have a list of questions as long as your arm? Nothing you've been puzzling over?"

Manjiro felt sweat trickle down his back. "I'm to be tarring the netting, sir," he said, glancing at Davis.

"Ah," Captain Whitfield said. "Has Mr. Davis barked at you already? Hmm. Now that you are a crew member, he'll treat you same as the others, I suspect."

He paused and Manjiro, not knowing what to say, kept quietly at his task.

"Well," the captain said, touching his cap, "I'm sure we'll have many opportunities for pleasant talk. I'm glad to see you aboard. I hope . . ." He trailed off and looked out to sea. "I hope it is a good journey."

Over the next few days, in his effort to avoid Jolly, Manjiro quickly learned every good hiding place onboard a ship. At every change of watch, he slipped into the galley, down the forecastle companionway, inside the trypots, or under a whaleboat, until he was sure it was safe to be seen.

But Jolly did not appear. Not at night and not during the day. This, it turned out, was more nerve-wracking than knowing where he was, and Manjiro's stomach worked itself into a tight knot.

After so many days of never seeing him, Manjiro started to relax. There were times that were a pleasure of wind and open water. He trimmed sails, coiled line, scrubbed the deck, and served the captain and the chief mates their meals.

He was taking a meal to the first mate one day when he overheard his shipmates talking.

"Where's Jolly, anyhow?" said one. "Why isn't he onboard?"

Manjiro set down his tray quietly.

"The night afore we was to ship out," Biscuit began conspiratorially, "Jolly took a dickey run and met his oppos. He was already half seas over by the time he hooked up with them and very shortly they was all three sheets in the wind."

What are they talking about? Manjiro wondered.

"That Jolly, he used to bleed the monkey, all right."

Isaiah nodded. "He was a shonkey, too."

Manjiro sighed. He would never understand English!

"Though I'm not entirely sure what all transpired," Biscuit went on. "Jolly had the devil to pay and no pitch hot."

What *were* they saying? Manjiro wondered. English was such a difficult language!

"Well, what happened?" Josiah said.

"I guess you can see which way the wind is blowin'," Biscuit said. "He either swallowed the anchor or slipped his cable!"

"Not so!" the mates cried, along with "Nay! You can't mean it!"

The clucking of tongues from the mates didn't help Manjiro to know what had happened to Jolly. Only that it wasn't good.

"Well, John Mung shouldn't miss him. Eh, Mung?" Suddenly, all eyes turned to look at him. "He used to cross yer bows enough."

But Manjiro was not happy. He was cold with remorse and guilt. Whatever had happened to Jolly, he knew he was responsible.

Later, in his bunk, he lay for a long time listening to the steady ticking of the captain's disk, like a chant, in his pocket. It told him he must, must, must go to the captain the next day, return the watch, and confess everything.

• • •

But the next morning he was sent straight from his bed to the masthead to "keep a weather eye out for whales."

He scrambled up the rigging and took his place high on the mainmast, standing on the two boards they called the "top-gallant crosstrees" and secured only by an iron hoop around his waist. After a time of gazing out at the glittering sea, he began to think about the silver disk weighing heavily in his pocket. He thought about how alone he was up there, and that perhaps he could take a good look at it, and try to figure out what it did. He might never again have such a chance.

With one arm looped around the mast to steady himself, Manjiro slid the watch from his pocket. He turned it over and over. He flipped open the cover. Was it a kind of charm? Did it give some kind of information, the way he had learned a compass did? There was only one thing to do: He would throw himself on the captain's mercy, take whatever punishment he deserved, and beg him to explain this curious device.

He was just shutting the lid when the ship lurched and the watch flew from his hand. He watched it sail out and down, turning and glinting in the bright sun. When he could no longer see it, Manjiro could only imagine the watch flipping and spinning, becoming just another bright fleck on the surface of the sea until, at last, it disappeared.

13

TREASURE

For several days, Manjiro went about his business deep in thought. On watch at night, he could barely look at the sky, for every star was like an eye, staring at him. Every wave tapping the boat nudged him; every groan of the ship was a reprimand. He knew he must go to the captain and confess everything, but he couldn't bring himself to do it. Once the captain knew how deceitful he'd been, and how incompetent—how by his own clumsiness he'd lost the captain's silver watch—the captain certainly wouldn't want anything to do with him!

One morning, Manjiro opened an eye to see the first mate, Mr. Davis, staring down at him. Manjiro jumped. In addition to his renowned temper, Manjiro's shipmates whispered that Mr. Davis was bit of a "Jack Nastyface."

"You're a lucky charm," Davis said.

"I'm a what?" Manjiro said.

"Since you've been aboard, we've been catching whales hand over fist."

"I don't think I—" Manjiro started to say, but Davis interrupted him.

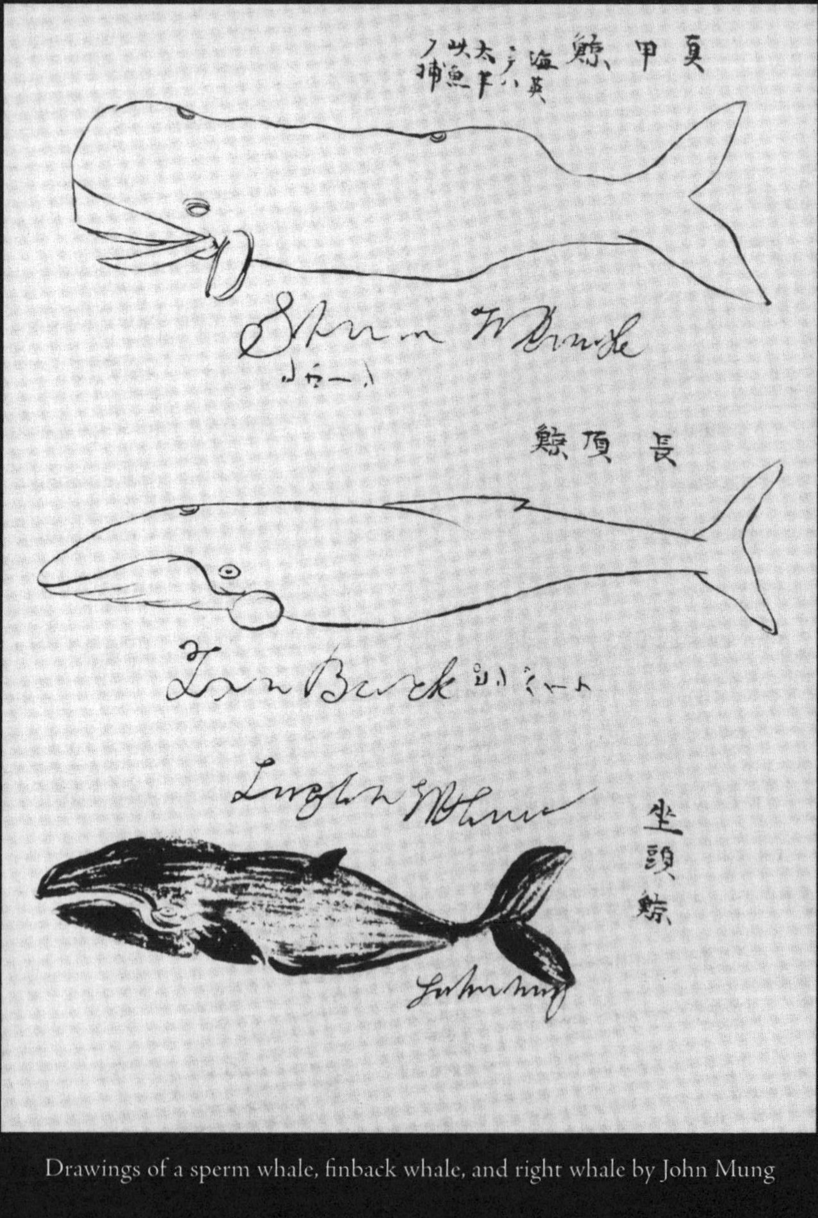

Drawings of a sperm whale, finback whale, and right whale by John Mung

"You know what treasure is?" he said.

Manjiro nodded. His shipmates told stories of pirates and their treasure. "Gold dubloons," he said.

"Aye, that's a certain kind of treasure," said Davis. "But that's not the kind I'm talking about."

"What kind, then?" Manjiro asked.

"Come along and find out," Davis said.

On deck, he saw that a whaleboat had been lowered and Biscuit stood in the boat, coiling a tow line. Davis and Manjiro scrambled into the boat, and each of them took up an oar.

The sea was still and silent except for the click and splash of oars. A pale mist rose off the water, and a curious smell permeated the air. The two men were perfectly quiet. There was none of the running banter or any of the urgency of the usual whale chase.

Manjiro wondered where they were going. Perhaps they were rowing to an island where pirates had buried gold and silver. Or to a cave stuffed with jewels. Wherever they were going, it stunk! The stench had grown so heavy, he began rowing with one hand so he could hold the other over his nose.

"Why is stink?" he said.

"Stink, you say?" Davis said. "Why, that's the heavenly smell of treasure."

It was a smell, all right. Manjiro felt as if he had to pull his oars against it, not just against the water.

"There she be!" Davis clapped his hands together. "And splendid to look upon, eh, Biscuit?"

"Aye," Biscuit replied, uncharacteristically quiet.

Emerging out of the mist was the sorriest looking whale Manjiro could imagine, so thin its ribs showed through its withered skin. Dead and rotting. That's what they'd been smelling.

"But," Manjiro said, "it so . . ." He couldn't think of the right word. "Dead."

"That is convenient indeed, for then we shan't need to kill her. Hook her up, Biscuit."

Biscuit hooked a tow line to the beast. "A right beauty," he said.

These men had lost their minds, Manjiro thought. He began to worry about being alone in this small boat with a couple of lunatics.

They rowed back to the ship, pulling the beast behind them. A group of hooting and laughing sailors gathered along the bulwark of the *John Howland*.

"Look here," one called out. "Mr. Davis and his crew has gone out and catched this leviathan by theirselves."

"Must have been a mighty struggle, was it, Mr. Davis?"

"Ye may make merry, ye lubbers," the first mate called to them, "but ye won't be laughin' long."

Biscuit stood by like a surgeon's assistant as Davis plunged his boat spade into the ruined whale's carcass. Mr. Davis shoveled away as if expecting to come upon a chest full of pirate gold. His face contorted into a red grimace; he grunted as he twisted the spade inside the beast. He's lost his wits, Manjiro thought.

The sailors along the bulwark grew quiet. A few of them shouted encouragement and even advice. Captain Whitfield appeared among the men and squinted down at the scene, a small smile playing on his lips.

Manjiro held his nose and wondered at this strangeness. It hardly seemed possible, but the smell seemed to get even worse, and everyone standing along the rail had grown silent and tense.

Then, like a freshening breeze, an entirely different and distinctly more pleasant smell wafted through the stench. Or at least, Manjiro thought, it was less unpleasant. At the same time, Mr. Davis held up a yellowish-gray glob. A cheer went up from the crew. They were *all* crazy, Manjiro thought.

"Treasure, lad!" Davis shouted.

"That does not look like treasure. It look like . . . like soybean paste!"

"That it may," Davis said, "but what matters more is what it does, for it's ambergris! What the druggist uses to make the finest of perfumes!"

"Worth a guinea an ounce, what say you to that?" Biscuit said, wiggling his furry eyebrows at Manjiro.

Manjiro had no idea what that meant, so he just wiggled his eyebrows in reply.

"I see you don't comprehend my meaning," Biscuit said. "A handful of that stuff will buy you a new wardrobe of fine suits and silk top hats."

"It'll buy you a nice house with glass windows," called out another mate.

"Buy you a whaleboat of your own," said another.

"Buy you a seat in Congress!" Biscuit cried, causing the crowd to roar.

Manjiro shook his head. So Davis hadn't been crazy after all. Surely, there was enough strangeness on this earth to last a lifetime. Already he'd seen huge floating mountains of ice, some with ships wrecked on them. He'd seen tusked bulls that swam in the ocean, dark red seals with horns at the tips of their muzzles, a huge star with a tail that filled the western sky, and rotted whales that gave up treasure. He supposed someday he'd see silk top hats, glass windows, and Congress seats, whatever those might be.

The sailors were turning away to get back to their business when Biscuit announced, "Say, mates, this must be what made old Mocha Dick so sick. Wouldn't you get a bellyache if you swallered this?"

Manjiro, along with the rest of the crew, turned to see what he had found.

Biscuit reached into the whale's belly and tugged at something. Then he held his arm out at full length and slowly opened his clenched fist. There, dangling from its slender chain, was the captain's silver watch.

14

THE HOUR OF THE DOG

During the first dog watch, most of the crew gathered on deck. The mood was merry. Enjoying a fair wind, the ship had moved away from the stench of the dead whale, and the setting sun filled the sky with red and purple streamers.

The captain stood near the mainmast, puffing on his pipe.

Manjiro put his head down and marched up to him. He'd resolved to tell the captain everything.

"John!" the captain greeted him enthusiastically. "You're so quiet these days. Do you regret your decision to come along?"

"No, sir!" Manjiro said. "No." He hung his head. Now was the time, he knew. He had to confess. "I am happy you get your watch back," Manjiro said quietly.

"As am I," the captain said.

"I know how it got there, in that whale," Manjiro said.

"Do you now?" The smoke from Captain Whitfield's pipe ascended like burning incense.

"I had it aloft," Manjiro said. "I look at it in the topgallant when I look for whales."

The captain turned to regard the boy. "How was it that you had it way up there? And why were you looking at it when you were supposed to be looking for whales?"

Manjiro hung his head. "Please excuse. I should be punished. I . . . I dropped it . . . into the sea."

The captain remained silent, puffing on his pipe. And everything rushed out of Manjiro—the story as best he could tell it: the attack by Jolly and the gang of thieves, the theft, and the fight. "I don't think you can believe," he finished. "Now it is my fault for Jolly not being here. I am sorry you lose your best harpooner and get me, only a greenhand."

The captain sighed and tapped his pipe against his hand. Then he did something Manjiro never would have expected: He laughed.

"Those fellows are clever, aren't they? They had us both fooled. You really thought that whale swallowed the watch, and I figured they filched my watch purely to play an elaborate joke on me." He shook his head but, glancing at Manjiro, frowned.

"Jolly was a troublemaker. Dishonest, too. I don't care for dishonesty on board my vessel . . . or anywhere." He looked pointedly at Manjiro. "I had already discharged him when he saw you. Perhaps he thought you were to blame. But you did nothing wrong . . . except looking at my watch when you were supposed to be watching for whales! I hope I don't hear of any further such slacking of your duties."

"No, sir," Manjiro said. "I look for whales."

"Now," the captain said, "here we've been together all this time and you haven't asked a single question. Surely you must have some question on your mind."

"Well . . . ," Manjiro said. "If watch not swallowed by whale, how did it get there?"

"Mr. Cooper," the captain shouted, and Biscuit dashed to his side. "Now tell us, where exactly did you find the watch? Let's have a straight answer, please. We'll keep your secret."

Biscuit leaned in toward them and whispered, "'Twas nestled like a diamond in the coils of a cobra, it was." He stood back, regarding them with an arched eyebrow and a knowing smirk.

Captain Whitfield thought. "A riddle now, is it?" he said. "Let's see . . . the diamond is the watch and the cobra would be a line . . . a line coiled in a tub, perhaps?" He looked up at the crosstrees, then down at the whaleboat they'd taken that morning. The captain slapped his thigh. "So that's it! The watch fell from the crosstrees into a whaleboat, and landed in a tub of line, which must have saved it. That was the line let out to tow the blasted whale, wasn't it?"

Drawing of a sailor on the ship's bow

Biscuit tipped his hat. "Aye, Captain. Yer wits be as sharp as a marlinspike."

He returned to his post, and Manjiro turned to the captain. "One other question, please," Manjiro said. "Is it a charm, the watch? What is it do?"

The captain explained to Manjiro how to tell time the Western way.

Manjiro explained that in his country people didn't carry watches. The passage of time was marked by the ringing of the temple bell at certain times of the day. At least, that was how it was done in his village. "The day," he said, "is divided into two pieces: sunrise to sunset and sunset to sunrise. Those are divided into six smaller pieces, like 'hours,' but instead of twenty-four, we have twelve. Each 'hour' has the name of an animal: tiger, rabbit, dragon, snake, horse, monkey, rooster. Now, I think, is the hour of the dog."

"That is interesting," Captain Whitfield said, "because we call this two-hour period of time the 'dog watch.'" He nodded to the sky, where the first stars were appearing. "Maybe we call it that because of that star." He pointed to a brilliant star and said, "That's Sirius, the dog star. Do you call it that?"

"No," said Manjiro. "We call that *Aoboshi,* blue star."

"'Tis blue, indeed," Captain Whitfield said, filling his pipe once more.

Manjiro smiled, for when the captain filled his pipe, it meant he intended to stay awhile longer. And that meant more conversation.

As each trembling star appeared, the captain and Manjiro found more to talk about, and the wind pushed them ever closer to their destination.

A drawing of New Bedford's waterfront by a Japanese artist. As the artist had never been to America, the landscape and buildings have a very Japanese sensibility.

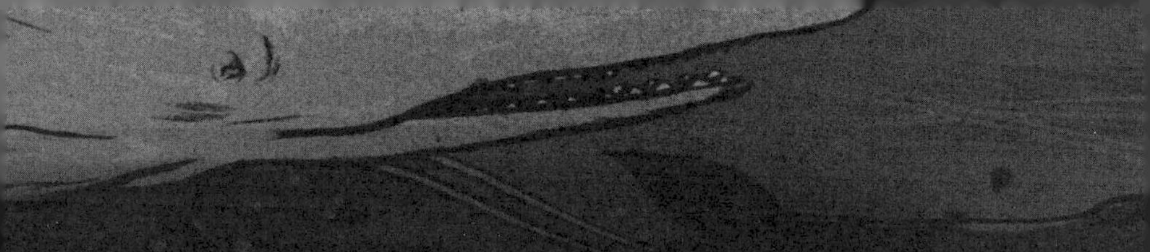

PART THREE
THE NEW WORLD

When one's own courage is fixed in his heart, and when his resolution is devoid of doubt, then when the time comes he will of necessity be able to choose the right move.

—from *Hagakure: The Book of the Samurai*

15

NEW BEDFORD AND FAIRHAVEN

May 7, 1843 (14th Year of Tempō, Year of the Hare)

After three-and-a-half years away, the *John Howland* pranced along the white foam of the sea toward home. All of her decks had been scrubbed to a shine, every brass knob buffed, every rail polished, and every flag on board fluttered from her rigging. She carried 2,761 barrels of whale oil and nineteen crew members, including one Japanese boy, for all anyone knew the first ever to come to America.

Manjiro was sixteen years old; he had been away from Japan for over two years, three-fourths of it spent on the sea. He had scrubbed himself shiny, trimmed his hair, and polished his boots. Then he stood at the foremast, waiting for the first glimpse of the shores of his new home.

But as the *John Howland* entered the mouth of the Acushnet River, the wind died and the ship was swallowed by a bank of white fog. Whaleboats were lowered and tow lines attached from the boats to the ship. For a while the only sound was the creaking and splashing of oars as the whaleboat crews towed the great vessel into the mist.

With the fog blotting out everything but the closest mast and shrouds, Manjiro felt as if he and his shipmates were adrift in the sky, surrounded by clouds—with no land anywhere and no other people on earth. His deck mates stood rigid and silent, straining their eyes for the dark shapes of land or the sudden, looming presence of another vessel.

Every few minutes, the ship's bell rang out, a lonely cry.

And then, as if in answer, came the solemn calling of the soundings: "Fifteen fathoms . . . eighteen fathoms . . ."

Presently, Manjiro became aware of a low buzzing hum, so low that he thought he imagined it. But the buzz grew more insistent, and then, one by one, distinct sounds began to jump out: Metallic rattling. Banging, followed by an echoing ring. Hollow clopping. The sudden shriek of a seagull. The shout of a human voice, then laughter. All these sounds drifted out over the water. As did the stench.

"What's that stink?" he said.

"'Tis the smell of an ocean's worth of whale oil, all tucked under a seaweed blanket," Captain Whitfield said, as he came to stand next to Manjiro. "You'll see."

Just then, the fog parted ahead of them, as if the *John Howland* herself had sliced it in two, revealing a strange and exotic world, swirling with color and motion.

Dozens of vessels crowded the harbor—whale ships, sloops, and schooners. Sail riggers crawled along the hundreds of masts and yards, tarring lines, bending on and hoisting sails. All along the wharf, painters slapped paint on boats, buildings, boards. Coopers shaped staves for oil casks, and packers packed barrels with hardtack. Horses pulled rattling carts past the thousands and thousands of seaweed-smothered oil casks that lined the wharf and snaked up the streets into the town. That explained the stench.

Manjiro had thought the port of Honolulu was a busy, crowded place, full of curious sights, but it was nothing but a couple of dusty streets compared to New Bedford.

He tried to gulp it in with his eyes. He felt as if he had flown over oceans and traveled through veils of fog and mist to arrive in a magical land of enchantment.

Tidy houses glittered up the hillside, punctuated by tall spires—tall as ships' masts.

People swarmed down the hills and through the streets. Boys skipped along, pushing hoops ahead of them with sticks. Women spun their parasols and lifted their skirts to avoid puddles. Some of them called out the names of loved ones—husbands, sons, fathers, brothers—who'd been away for years.

There is no one waiting for me, Manjiro thought, then

stole a glance at Captain Whitfield. The captain's gaze seemed to go out beyond the farthest house, the farthest hill. There was no one waiting for him, either.

"You miss your wife," Manjiro said.

Captain Whitfield nodded. "And you miss your mother. But you and I, we are a family now."

After the barrels had been unloaded and the owners of the *John Howland* had proclaimed themselves satisfied with its impressive cargo, Manjiro and Captain Whitfield walked down the gangplank and stepped onto American soil. This was a moment Manjiro had long imagined. He'd imagined himself striding confidently into his new life, but his legs were now so unsteady from the many months at sea that he wove about like a drunken man.

As Captain Whitfield stopped to speak to someone, Manjiro clung to a railing and gazed out at the town. Women swished by, with skirts so full they could have hidden a giant sea turtle under them. The men's long-tailed coats made them look like elegant birds as they picked their way among the barrels in the streets. Manjiro was thrilled. It was a beautiful place, America, even if it did stink of whale oil. It was a land filled with lovely people and truly full of wonders! He could not look at enough things at once.

Then he had the distinct feeling that someone was looking

at *him*. He turned to see a row of boys about his own age slouched against the wall of a building, staring at him. One of the boys said something behind his hand and the others snickered. Manjiro's heart sank a little; he could tell they were laughing at him. It wouldn't all be wondrous, he supposed, and he was grateful when the captain whisked him away down the street.

Everywhere they went, they stopped to chat with people. Captain Whitfield introduced Manjiro to so many people that his head spun. With each new person he had to resist the impulse to bow and remember instead to extend his right hand in greeting.

While Captain Whitfield made some purchases, Manjiro marveled at the goods displayed in each of the shops' big windows. On display were harpoons, hammocks, candles, lanterns . . . everything a whaling ship might need.

As he ogled the fancy cakes in the baker's window, he was startled by his reflection in the glass. How odd he looked, in his Western clothes! A movement, also reflected in the glass, caught his eye, and his gaze shifted behind him to a handful of boys—the same boys he'd seen earlier. He watched quietly as the boys made faces and rude gestures behind his back. One pulled at his eyelids, making his eyes into ugly slits in his face. Another bowed and bobbed. The other boys doubled over laughing.

Is this how he looked to people—strange and grotesque?

Did everyone see him this way?

As he was contemplating this, the boys abruptly stopped and looked at something. Manjiro followed their gazes and noticed a finely dressed man shaking his gold-handled walking stick at them.

"You scoundrels should be ashamed of yourselves!" he snapped. "Haven't you anything better to do? Off with you, or I shall have your hides!"

The boys scattered and the man winked at Manjiro. Then he continued up the hill, whistling and casually swinging his walking stick.

Captain Whitfield reappeared and Manjiro said, "Do you know that man?"

The captain squinted at the receding figure. "No," he said.

"Why would he do a kindness to me?" Manjiro asked.

"Why shouldn't he?"

"Because I am just a boy and he is a grown person. I am a poor nobody and he is a rich important person."

"And why can't a rich man be kind to a poor 'nobody'?"

Manjiro didn't have an answer. He was as puzzled by the man's kindness as by the boys' cruelty.

"Well!" Captain Whitfield said, clapping his hands together. "Let's go home, shall we? First thing we'll do is get a little fire going to take the chill off the place and then fix ourselves some supper." He patted the packages he carried under his arm and steered Manjiro toward the long bridge that led to Fairhaven, the town on the other side of the Acushnet River. Manjiro had noticed this bridge from the *John Howland*—it broke in two so that vessels could pass through, then closed shut again, so that people could pass over it. He planned to draw a picture of it as soon as he got the chance.

Dusk had fallen and a cold drizzle was falling by the time they rounded the corner to the captain's house. Still, Captain Whitfield whistled the final few blocks. "Soon there!" he said. Manjiro felt his heart drumming in his chest—partly from the long walk, but mostly in anticipation. Soon he would see his new home.

Suddenly the whistling stopped, and coming up behind the captain, Manjiro saw the reason. The house before them was shuttered, the windows covered over with wide boards. Weeds and vines clung to its walls and cobwebs to the downspout.

"No one has cared for your house!" Manjiro blurted out.

After the fatigue of the day and now without prospect of a bed, Manjiro felt a wave of loneliness wash over him. He wondered if his home in Japan was similarly empty and unkempt. The gray clouds and mist that shrouded the roofs of the town seemed to settle on his shoulders.

The captain lowered himself slowly to sit on the front step, and Manjiro sat down next to him. They picked at the tall grass that grew up around the steps, tearing off little bits and tossing them in the yard. Finally, Captain Whitfield sighed and said, "This was not the homecoming I envisioned for you."

"It's all right," Manjiro said. "You and me, we family now."

Captain Whitfield's dark look blew away like a squall's black clouds. He smiled. "That's exactly right," he said. "We've got each other now. We may have had our sails knocked back, but only for a moment, for there's Mr. and Mrs. Aken's house—you know their son Isaachar, who you called Itchy. Why, and there's Eben himself."

A man had come out on the stoop of the house. He looked their way and shouted, "Is that my good friend William Whitfield sitting there looking so forlorn? Please come out of the damp and the cold. There's supper and a bed here!"

Mrs. Aken dished up bowls of steaming chowder. Later, Manjiro climbed a number of creaking stairs to go to bed. In spite of the many novelties of the day, he hadn't been able to shake the dark gloom he'd felt earlier, seeing the captain's empty house and thinking of those boys who'd made fun of him—snickering and pulling at the edges of their eyes to make their faces into grotesque masks. Now, listening to the rain slashing against the windows and the wind whistling through the sashes, he wondered if Goemon had been right. What if his decision had been a horrible mistake?

But soon the rain and wind began to take on the rhythm of the sea, and pulling up the warm quilt and sinking into the soft bed, he fell asleep and dreamed he was once again aboard ship, surging toward a splotch of brilliant sunshine.

The next morning, Manjiro crept down the creaking wooden stairs, trying not to disturb anyone who might be sleeping. He heard soft voices in the kitchen, which he recognized as Captain Whitfield's and Mr. and Mrs. Aken's.

He paused, not wanting to disturb them, and heard the captain say, "I had resigned myself to a life at sea, with a small house in Fairhaven for my few months between ships. But now, with a bright young ward, I've begun to think of a farm again. A boy should have land to roam, work for his hands to do, a pond to fish, and a horse to ride."

Who was this boy they were talking about? Was it him? Was the captain suggesting that *he* should have a *horse* to ride?

"And a mother?" Mrs. Aken said.

"Aye," Captain Whitfield said. "A boy needs a mother."

"And a man needs a wife," said Mr. Aken.

Manjiro did not feel he needed another mother, but it

might not be so bad to have an American one. He glanced out the small window on the landing where he stood. The tiny spring leaves were polished bright with sunlight. His dark mood of the previous night had dissolved.

"If I'm not mistaken," Mrs. Aken went on, "there is someone that you care for, isn't there?"

Captain Whitfield mumbled into his cup of coffee.

"Well . . . ?" Mr. Aken said.

"I thought it all out on the journey home," the captain said, "and I have a plan."

Soon after, Captain Whitfield told Manjiro he was going to New York on business. Manjiro would stay with Mr. and Mrs. Aken.

"Is New York where you go to get a wife or a mother?" Manjiro said.

Captain Whitfield looked at him with one quizzical eye and burst out laughing.

"So you overheard our conversation, did you? I hope you know that it is impolite to eavesdrop."

Manjiro hung his head. "I am sorry to eaves drip."

"Eavesdrop," the captain corrected. "There's no harm done. And it is true that there is a lady of whom I am quite fond.

She's as fine and prudent a woman as any in all of the eastern seaboard, or anywhere, and I tell you, I am resolved to have her for a wife."

"If you like her, then I like her, too," Manjiro said, determined to make it true.

"You deserve a proper upbringing, John, and you shall have it." Captain Whitfield adjusted his cap on his head, touched his fingers to the brim as if in a salute, and was gone.

16

SAMURAI FARM BOY

Captain Whitfield returned from his trip to New York with his new wife, Albertina. Her face crinkled up so much when she smiled that her twinkly blue eyes almost disappeared in her round cheeks. She smiled a lot, and Manjiro liked her right away.

A farm was procured; a fine house built, with many rooms, glass windows, and carpets made out of the wool of sheep. Manjiro had a room to himself, with land to roam and farm animals to tend, a stream to fish, and—just like a real samurai—a horse to ride, a pleasure he never would have been allowed in Japan. Like a character in a fairy tale, Manjiro found himself transformed from a poor fisherman into a prince . . .

. . . the kind of prince who had chores. He weeded the garden, fed chickens, gathered eggs, milked the cow, and tended to many other tasks that filled up his summer days. When his chores were done, he rode his horse, Plum Duff, around the farm, along the lane, across fallow fields, into the oak woods, or down to the stream to fish.

He fell off in all those places, too. If Plum Duff changed gaits, Manjiro would jounce off her back. If she came to a stop too fast, he'd slide up and over her head. At a trot, he'd bounce so much that eventually he'd bounce right off. He landed on country roads, plunked down into meadows, crashed into fields, plopped into streams, and splatted into mud puddles.

Falling off Plum Duff was how Manjiro met Terry. Once, when he had done a somersault over her head and landed on his back in a field of alfalfa, he looked up to see a face peering down at him—a face wearing an almost comical look of surprise. The boy the face belonged to carried a fishing pole over one shoulder and a small wicker basket over the other.

"Havin' a nap?" the boy, Terry, said.

"I fell off my horse," Manjiro said.

"What horse?" Terry said.

Manjiro sat up. Plum Duff was nowhere to be seen. Manjiro stood, wobbling a little. He must have been knocked out cold for her to get so far away that he couldn't see her anymore.

"Plum Duff!" he hollered. "Plum Duff!"

"What kind of name is that for a horse?" Terry asked.

"Plum Duff—it is best food on whale ship," Manjiro said.

"Oh, you mean plum duff."

"That's what I said."

"No, you said 'prumuduffu.'"

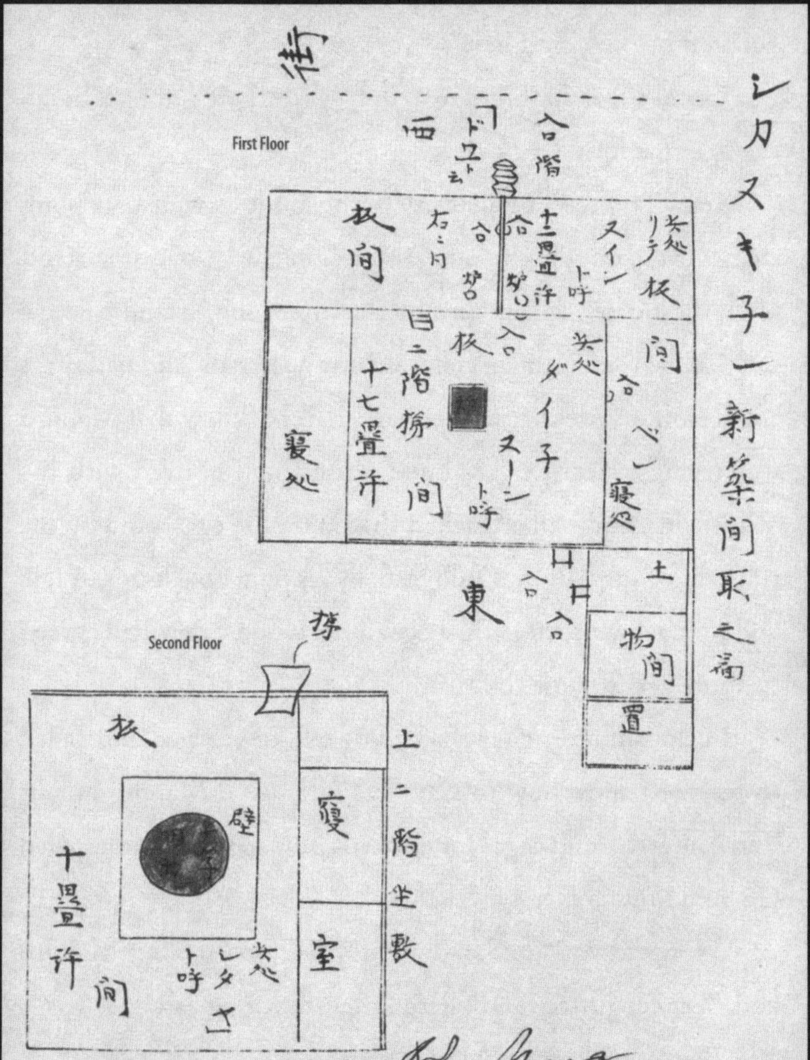

The floor plan of Captain Whitfield's house drawn by John Mung

"Whatever you want to call the horse, I don't mind, but will you help me find her?"

"Sure, I'll help, but I'm telling you, there's got to be an easier name for your horse."

Terry pointed out a silvery path, about as wide as a pony, that wove through the alfalfa, and the two boys struck off after the horse. By the end of the afternoon, Manjiro knew that Terry lived in town, collected stray animals, and had three small trout inside that wicker basket. Terry knew that Manjiro was trying to learn to read and write English, lived with the Whitfields, and had a chicken that laid blue eggs. And by the time they found Plum Duff casually ripping up clumps of tall, wide-bladed grass near the edge of the woods, they had agreed to shorten the name to Duffy.

In the summer days that followed, Terry tried and failed to teach Manjiro how to stay on Duffy. And Manjiro taught Terry how to build cages for crickets, how to play a game called Go, and how to filet a fish.

"How did you learn to do that?" Terry asked after Manjiro had cleaned, gutted, and filleted their morning catch.

"Don't you know how to filet fish?"

"Not like that—so clean and fast."

"The key is to have a sharp knife," Manjiro said, "as sharp as a samurai's sword."

"A sama-what?"

Manjiro explained as best he could that, in his country, people were born into their rank, and that "Samurai are very high-status people who are trained in all manner of fighting, including swords-ship."

"Swordsmanship?" Terry corrected.

"But my country hasn't had battles in more than two hundred years, so samurai now don't have much to do. But samurai of long ago times, they make legends of themselves."

On their way home from the fishing hole, the boys walked through a meadow, swatting at the tall grass with sticks while grasshoppers flung themselves out of their way.

"A samurai's sword should be sharp enough to slice through a floating water lily, but strong enough to cut through seven corpses," Manjiro said matter-of-factly.

"*Ka-zing!*" Terry cried, taking a swipe at a pesky fly.

"No, not like that," Manjiro said. "Like this." He showed Terry some sword-fighting moves like the "zigzag," "reverse dragonfly," "waterwheel," and "eight-sides-at-once." These were real names for styles of swordplay, but he and his friends back home didn't really know what they meant; they just made up their own moves. Then Manjiro told Terry about the different kinds of swords and knives, including the *katana,* the *nodachi,* the *tanto,* and the *naginata.* He didn't tell Terry that he never would have been allowed to actually carry a sword.

"If you went back to Japan would you be a samurai?" Terry said.

Manjiro hesitated before answering. He could explain that there was no possible way he could ever be a samurai, that if he went back to Japan he would be a simple fisherman again. That he really didn't know anything about swords or about swordplay—it was all made up by boys in his village so remote from actual samurai that they could get away with such foolishness. But he didn't. Instead, he said, "Yes. That's what I would be."

"Ooh," Terry said. "That would be something."

"It would," Manjiro said. "It really would be something."

17

FITTING IN

For a while the differences between life in America and life in Japan were always on Manjiro's mind. If only he could write! He would record the strange and wonderful things he observed in America. He would write it all in a letter to his mother, tuck it into an envelope, and stash it in the little box where he kept small treasures—the dozens of shells he had collected from all the places he'd been. Until then, he tucked his letters away in his memory.

Time is different here. There is no such thing as a tiger year, rat year, dragon year, and so on. There are twenty-four hours in a day and a year is divided into twelve months.

People greet each other by extending their right hands.

They like to sing and often do this when walking down roads.

A kind of sweet juice runs from the trees. It is so sweet, sugar is made from it.

The fronts of shops are made of glass, so a person passing by can look in and see all the splendid things.

Ordinary men carry timepieces called "watches." When walking they carry canes, inside of which swords are often hidden.

They make a wonderful food out of flour and salt and eggs and water. It is called "bread."

The fields are so large, the farmers have to use horses to sow the wheat.

Ordinary people can become as wealthy as emperors. They live in houses as large and richly decorated as palaces.

In this land, everyone has two names, instead of just one like common people do at home.

In the United States they call a temple a "church." The priest has a wife and children and they all eat meat. Churches are large and often have a clock on the tower. Many people gather with their books and the priest stands on a high platform and tells the people to open their books to certain pages. The priest reads from these pages and then explains the meaning.

At church on Sunday morning, Manjiro tried to concentrate on the minister and what he was saying from his high pulpit, but the stifled coughs and frowning faces of the church elders distracted him. They didn't approve of him. What was wrong? he wondered.

He touched his hair—clean and soft. He brushed at his jacket and ran a finger under his tight, starched collar; it was clean and stiff. He'd gotten used to bathing only occasionally, as the Westerners did, and he was as clean as anybody else in this church. He sniffed at the sleeves of his jacket. He couldn't possibly smell any worse than old Mr. Wasser, two pews up, who reeked of tobacco and sauerkraut.

The next week the Whitfields went to a different church. But it was the same thing there. People who were polite to him on the street pouted when they saw him at church. The elders frowned and the ladies pursed their lips and adjusted their bonnets.

Manjiro kept his head bowed most of the time, just like he had in Japan. There he did it because he was a poor fisherman. Practically anybody's status was higher than his. But here, he was the son of a well-to-do whaling captain. That should have put him in a higher status, almost the highest. So he was puzzled that the men scowled and the ladies sniffed.

As he pondered this, the little girl in the pew ahead of him turned to look at him. She stared—as children did everywhere—with simple curiosity. Ah! Manjiro realized. It was just the way he looked. He'd forgotten he looked funny to people. If people met him on the street, he was a delightful novelty. They fussed over him as if he were a monkey one of the whalers had brought from some tropical place. Sometimes he wondered if they expected him to do a backflip, then hold out a tin cup. In a church, however, apparently the way he looked was an offense.

After the service, Manjiro stood with Mrs. Whitfield as she chatted with friends, but his eye was on the captain and two of the church deacons, who stood apart from them. From where he stood, Manjiro had a good view of the captain's face, and he could read it the way he'd learned to read the ocean and its weather—its dark clouds, fair breezes, raging storms. At first the captain's face showed open friendliness, but when one of the other men glanced toward Manjiro, the captain's countenance turned dark and steely. The look he gave the deacons—a slight tightening of the jaw, the eyebrow raised over his one open eye, slightly pursed lips—was one he might wear if the crew were slow to bring the ship about or let the sails luff or lie back. When Manjiro saw a vein pulsing in his neck, he knew something was really raising the captain's ire. Although Manjiro had heard him give sharp orders, he had never heard him raise his voice in anger, and he didn't do it now, either. The deacons, seemingly unaware of how angry Captain Whitfield was, touched their fingers to the brims of their hats and retreated into the church.

After the two men had gone, Captain Whitfield strode over to Mrs. Whitfield and Manjiro and swept them both away.

"What happened with those church elders?" Manjiro asked.

"Those 'elders' think you 'would be more comfortable in the seats reserved for negroes,'" Captain Whitfield said.

"More comfortable?" Manjiro said.

"It's ridiculous!" the captain said firmly. He clamped his jaw tight, and Manjiro knew the conversation was over.

The next Sunday, when Mrs. Whitfield came to his room to wake him for church, Manjiro pulled the covers up to his nose and coughed.

"I think I'm a little sick," he said.

"Too sick to go to church?" Mrs. Whitfield said.

Manjiro nodded.

She pressed the back of her hand to his forehead and looked at his eyes. "No fever." She sat down on a chair across from his bed. "Perhaps you just don't *want* to go to church?"

Manjiro didn't answer.

Mrs. Whitfield raised an eyebrow.

"I don't mind church!" Manjiro blurted out. "But I bring unhappiness to people there. I cause them to be . . . ," Manjiro didn't know any other word to describe it. "Unhappy."

"You do no such thing!" said Mrs. Whitfield. "They cause their own unhappiness."

"But it's me they don't like. They don't want me there."

"Oh, they don't mind you being there," Mrs. Whitfield

said. "It's just that they want you to sit in the pew for colored people."

"I don't mind sitting there, you know. Especially if it will make people happier," Manjiro said. "I will do that."

"It won't make anybody happier, and you will do no such thing," said Mrs. Whitfield. "The very idea! Why there should be such a thing as a separate pew for colored people—honestly! And in a place of worship that claims to believe in equality for all. I hope we live to see the day when such notions are abolished—along with our country's deplorable institution of slavery. There's a movement, you know, gaining momentum. Now, get up, John, we're not going to that church anymore. William has found a different church where they believe as we do that all men—*all* men—are created equal."

"And women?" Manjiro asked.

"Ah, yes," said Mrs. Whitfield. "That is yet another question to be addressed, isn't it? There's a movement for more rights for women, too. So much happening these days. The country is suffering growing pains, just like some boys around here. Now, are you going to lie abed on such a morning as this? Or are you going to get up and help the world change—starting with our religious institutions?"

At church, Manjiro tried to concentrate on the preacher's sermon and the words of the hymns, but Mrs. Whitfield's words had stuck in his head. *Are you going to get up and help the world change?*

It was not something he'd ever thought was possible before. Or at least, he had not thought that *he* would ever be able to bring change to the world.

In Japan, nothing ever seemed to change. Life went on in the same way it had for hundreds of years. But here, things were changing constantly—people buzzed with talk of a way to send messages clear across the country in a few moments; of iron boxes that ran on tracks and moved so fast that people said time itself would be obliterated. Someone had to be making all these things happen. Someone had to be changing the world. What if *he* could be one of those people?

18

SCHOOL

School was where it would all begin. Manjiro had never been to school. He didn't know how to read and write even his own language. Now he was going to learn to read and write in English, and to do that, he would have to attend class with the little children. Sixteen-year-old boys like him went to different schools. If they were smart enough, they could go to the Bartlett School of Navigation. That place was for students who excelled in school, who were likely to go on to be whaling captains, ship owners, important people. At Bartlett they could learn mathematics, surveying, and, most important, all the secrets of navigation. That was the school Manjiro longed to attend.

But he began his education at the Stone House School, where he studied arithmetic, learned the alphabet, worked at reading and writing English, and practiced a thing called penmanship.

When he wasn't in school, he helped Captain Whitfield with the chores. They cut and baled hay together, harvested vegetables, milked the cows, and put up fencing.

It was sometimes comical to see the mighty Captain

Whitfield with a pitchfork in his hand, mucking out the cow's stall or turning dirt over with a spade. But the captain seemed to enjoy farming almost as much as sailing. Almost.

In the evening, Manjiro and Captain Whitfield sat on the porch and discussed the events of the day. It was, Manjiro thought, a lot like the way they had stood together at the bulwark of the *John Howland,* talking into the night, their words given to the darkness for safekeeping.

One evening, the captain cleared his throat and said, "Miss Allen tells me you can't go to her school anymore."

"I can't?" Manjiro said. "Did I do something wrong?"

"No," Captain Whitfield chuckled, "nothing wrong—you've just learned everything there is to learn at that school. You need to go to a different one."

Now Manjiro's heart pounded in his chest. "What school?" he asked.

"Well . . . I spoke to Mr. Bartlett about his academy. . . ."

Manjiro could hardly hear for the roar in his ears.

"He wasn't sure you were the right material for that school."

Manjiro's stomach clenched.

"But . . . ," the captain went on, "I told him how well you'd done at Miss Allen's school—they say you 'fairly soak up learning'—and what a bright, motivated student you are, and he agreed to give you a try."

Manjiro leaped up, shook the captain's hand, and ran inside and hugged Mrs. Whitfield.

"Now, sit down, John," Captain Whitfield said when the boy returned. "I'm not finished."

Manjiro sat down—on the edge of his chair.

"Mr. Bartlett has agreed to give you a try *with some conditions*. You have to be able to keep up with the other students; your English must be up to his standards—reading, writing, and speaking—and you can't get into any mischief."

"Mischief?"

"Trouble. He doesn't want any trouble on your account."

"Aye, aye, sir!" Manjiro said. "No trouble!"

19

VICTORY WITHOUT FIGHTING

A current had drawn him toward this moment—a current as strong as *Kuroshio* had pulled him to Captain Whitfield and to America and now to the Bartlett School. Nothing was going to stop him from learning everything he could, especially about how to navigate the world's oceans. He was going to study hard. He was going to use good English and correct grammar and work hard on his spelling. He was going to pay attention to the teacher, not ask too many questions, and above all, he was not going to get into trouble.

He arrived early his first day. As he stood waiting for the school to open, he noticed a shiny coin on the ground in front of him. What, he wondered, was the right thing to do? Surely he couldn't just pick it up and keep it for himself? Or could he? Someone had lost this coin. Perhaps whoever had lost it would come back and look for it. He should probably leave it.

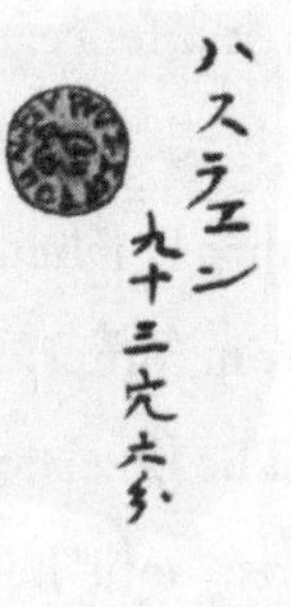

Half dime drawn by John Mung

But what if someone came along and took it? Wouldn't it be better if he tried to find the owner? Manjiro decided this would be the right course of action, and he bent to pick it up. But just as his fingers were about to close around it, the coin skittered out of his reach!

That was odd, he thought, and he tried once more. But again, just as he was about to pick it up, the coin scooted away as if it were alive!

Manjiro stared at the coin. There it lay on the ground, unmoving, just as you would expect it to do.

This time, he decided, he would step on it to prevent it from skittering away. He inched his foot toward it, and gradually lifted the toe of his shoe. He was just bringing it down when the coin jumped out from under his foot.

What would make it do such a thing?

Manjiro stood back and scratched his chin. He gave the coin a good, hard look, and for the first time noticed the very fine thread attached to it. Looking up, he noticed a tall boy leaning against a fence, calmly chewing on a stalk of grass. But behind that blade of grass, the boy couldn't quite conceal a smirk. Manjiro laughed and said, "That is a good joke. Are you making the coin jump?"

The boy shook his head, then jerked his thumb toward the woods. "Job!" he shouted. "You've been found out."

A willowy boy wearing a bemused smile appeared from behind a tree. "I fooled you, huh?" he said, winding the thread around a stick as he walked.

"You must be some kind of dupe," the boy at the fence said, sneering at Manjiro.

Manjiro recognized this boy. He was one of the boys who had made faces behind his back that very first day in America. Now he was in on some kind of joke that was being played at Manjiro's expense.

"What is a 'dupe'?" Manjiro said.

The boy snickered. "It's what you are: stupid."

Job said, "Sheesh, Tom, ease up a little."

Manjiro turned to the boy named Job. "That is a pretty good joke. But you can fool more clever people than me if you use different string. If you want a suggestion, of course."

"Sure," Job scratched at his mop of hair. "What kind of string?"

Manjiro picked up the coin, and was about to open his mouth when the tall boy spat out his grass and pushed himself away from the fence.

"Job!" he said, loudly, for the benefit of some other students who had begun to gather. "You're not really going to listen to this squinty-eyed son of a pig are you?"

Job looked from Manjiro to the tall boy and back again. "Well, Tom, I . . . ," he said.

Tom walked up to Manjiro and glared down at him. Tom was bigger and taller than Manjiro, and maybe older, too. But Manjiro's many months on a whale ship had made him tough and strong. He might be able to beat Tom if it came to a fight.

A truly strong person does not resort to violence unless it absolutely cannot be avoided, Manjiro reminded himself. His father had taught him that. Manjiro also remembered what Captain Whitfield had said about staying out of trouble.

Manjiro stepped around Tom.

Or he tried to. Tom put his hand on Manjiro's chest and said, "Do you really think you are going to this school? *This* school? *You?*"

Manjiro didn't answer. Victory without fighting, Manjiro reminded himself, was honorable.

"See?" Tom said to a cluster of boys behind him—his friends? "He don't even understand what I'm saying. He's not smart enough for that."

Other students who were arriving for school, both boys and girls, hung back.

"I don't think you're going to fit in here. I don't think we let people like *you* into *this* school," Tom said. He crossed his arms and stood in Manjiro's way. A few students walked around them, up the stairs and into the school, but when Manjiro tried to move one way or the other, Tom would move, too, blocking his way.

"Go home, little slant-eyes," Tom said. "Go home where you came from."

If only I could, Manjiro thought, I would. There was a long pause while Manjiro wondered what to do. Then he remembered he still had the coin in his hand.

Tom seemed to remember that at the same time, because he said, "Give me back my two bits, punk."

"I know a coin trick, too," Manjiro said. He pulled the thread off the coin and tossed the coin high in the air. He felt all eyes shift to focus on it—even the students on the steps turned back to watch. The coin spun back down, winking in the sun. Manjiro caught it, simultaneously catching the eye of a girl who stood nearby. He felt his face flush.

"That's no trick!" Tom said.

"He hasn't done it yet, Tom," the girl said.

Manjiro tried not to think about the girl as he wove the coin through the fingers of his right hand the way Itch had taught him. He would look very foolish if he didn't pull this off, he knew, and he focused all his concentration on the trick.

Next, he pinched the coin between the thumb and forefinger of his right hand, holding it so all could see. Then, with a big flourish, he placed—or seemed to place—the coin in his left hand.

"Abracadabra!" he said, making a sweeping gesture toward that hand. "Vanish!" He curled open the fingers of his left hand to reveal his empty palm.

"Oh!" the girl exclaimed, clapping her hands. "That was a good trick!"

"He's stolen it, is all," Tom said. "And he better give it back, 'cuz it's mine!"

The schoolmaster came to the door and stood with his arms folded, taking in the scene with a stern look.

Manjiro glanced at him, trying to determine if he was in trouble already. He had to make the coin reappear to complete the trick, so he forged on.

"Now I make it appear!" Manjiro started to reach toward the girl's face, intending to make the coin seem to come out of her ear. That was the way the trick was supposed to work. But he stopped, his arm suspended in midair. What if he accidentally touched her! Something like this could never happen in Japan, he suddenly thought—for a man and woman to be so familiar in public! But he was not in Japan, he reminded himself—he was in America now, where men and women walked arm in arm on the street. Manjiro's hand brushed against the girl's hair, his heart leaped into his throat, and he almost dropped the coin. But he finished the trick smoothly. Perhaps nobody even noticed the hesitation. The students broke out into applause, and the girl touched her ear. "Is there anything else in there?" she laughed.

"I see we have a magician in our midst," Mr. Bartlett said. "Now, would you all kindly enter so we can begin classes?"

The students filed in, still chattering about the trick. "How did you do that?" a boy asked.

"Do it again!" said another boy.

"Pah!" Tom spat. "That's nothing. I know lots of tricks like that."

"No, you don't, Tom," Job said. "I've never seen you do any tricks at all."

Manjiro followed the other students into the school. He could just see the back of the girl's head, and he kept his eyes on her glossy brown hair swishing back and forth.

He was not so naïve as to think the coin trick would put an end to Tom's taunts. The best way to win this fight would be to succeed in school—at least he had to make it through this one day.

Manjiro made it through that day and another and another. Most of the students accepted him just fine. After discussing the trick, Manjiro gave Job a length of fishing line that would be even harder to see than sewing thread. Soon Job was spending time with Terry and Manjiro, and sometimes he helped out at the Whitfield farm.

But the more friends Manjiro made and the better he did in school, the more Tom and his friends seemed to dislike him.

"I don't see why one of *those* people should be allowed in our school," Tom said out loud when the teacher had stepped out of the classroom for a moment. "His people would just as soon kill you as look at you."

"My dad says they go about with giant swords and will chop open your head like a watermelon," said one of Tom's friends.

"How do we know he's not a spy?" Tom said. "That's what I think. He's been sent here to spy on us and report back to his government."

"Oh, yeah, Tom," Job said, his voice dripping with sarcasm. "I'm sure his government is extremely interested in our particular geometry class."

"You shut your trap, Job," Tom snapped. "People are going to think you're anti-American if you keep being friends with him. There's no way he'll ever really be American. He shouldn't be allowed in this school. We shouldn't have to go to school with people who want to kill us."

"Stow it, Tom," someone in the back called out.

"You stow it or I'll come back there and make you," Tom yelled back.

"Yeah?"

"You know I will."

A fight was narrowly avoided when the teacher reentered. The boys abruptly sat down, and the teacher gave them all a withering glance before continuing.

20

THE CHALLENGE

Winter was quiet. The wind and cold kept people bundled up in thick overcoats and woolen scarves, hurrying from one warm stove to the next. At school there were lessons and reading and tests, and Tom and the others were too busy to tease and bully. But spring brought green leaves, fishing, and fresh taunts.

"I thought Tom was finished griping at you," Terry said as the three friends sat on the bank of the stream, fishing. "But I guess not." The stream chuckled along, untouched by any such unpleasantness.

"Aw, he's always got to pick on somebody," Job said. "I used to be friends with him just so he wouldn't pick on me."

"I don't know what I can do about it," Manjiro said. He cast; his line went into the water with a *plink,* and then all was silent as the boys contemplated what he might do.

"Maybe you should take the offensive." Terry made a face as he gingerly pulled a worm out of a small tin of bait, as if he were startled to find a worm there. Manjiro laughed at the look on his friend's face—somehow Terry was able to look disgusted and surprised at the same time.

"Yeah!" Job said. "Challenge him to a fight or something."

"A fistfight!" Terry said. He gave up trying to bait his hook, threw the worm into the woods, lay back, and pushed his hat over his eyes.

"Are you crazy?" Job said. "Do you ever *look* at Tom? He's always got a black eye or a cut on his face. They say he's so tough, he picks fights with whaling men."

Terry emitted a low whistle. "Really? Well, then, you'll never beat him at a fistfight."

"I don't want to have a fistfight with him!" Manjiro said. "Why would I? I can't get into trouble. I might get throwed out of school."

"Thrown," Terry corrected. Then he jumped up. "Gee whiz, Johnny Mung, I know what you should do! You should fight him with swords. You'd surely win then. Nobody around here knows such fancy moves. So what do you say? Should I set it up with you and him and swords?" He swung his fishing pole around his head to demonstrate.

"Hey, watch it! There's a hook on that!" Job said. Terry stopped swinging.

"Swords?" Manjiro said. "A sword fight would definitely get me throwed—thrown—out of school. Another thing—

when people fight with those kinds of swords, somebody's head is sure to come off."

"Really?" Job said. "Somebody's whole head gets cut off?"

As the boys walked back to the farm, Manjiro explained how the samurai swords were so ferocious that their strength was tested by slicing up corpses. He said stories were told of men who had been severed from shoulder to hip so quickly that they walked on for several paces before splitting in two. A sword like that took a head off in one swoop. "But they say that even after a man's head has been cut off, he can still perform some function," Manjiro said.

"Like what kind of function, do you think?" Job said.

"Sometimes chickens run around after their heads are chopped off," Terry said.

"That may be, but chickens don't know any better," Job said. "If a person's head were cut off, he would know it; he'd know he was supposed to fall down dead. His brain would say, 'Look there; your head is gone! You're dead! Fall down!'"

"But what if there was something he wanted to do before dying? Perhaps a body could stand up long enough to do that one thing," Manjiro said.

"But the brain isn't connected anymore—how can it tell the body what to do?" Terry asked.

"Maybe it told the body what to do already, so the body knew it ahead," Manjiro said.

"Like what? What could it do?"

"Kill the person who cut off his head," Job said, slashing the air with his stick.

"Or wave good-bye!" Terry giggled.

As they walked into the farmyard, Mrs. Whitfield poked her head around a sheet hanging on the clothesline. "What *are* you talking about?" she said.

"Sorry, Mrs. Whitfield," Terry said. "We're just trying to figure out a challenge for John and Tom."

"A challenge?" she said.

"A sword fight won't work," Job grumbled.

"That's good to know," Mrs. Whitfield said. "What is this challenge about?"

"Nothing!" Manjiro said hastily. He hadn't noticed her hanging clothes or he would have ended the conversation. "We're just . . . we're just talking."

"Tom is always picking on John," Terry said. "We thought if he could beat him up somehow, he'd stop."

Mrs. Whitfield stood up from the clothes basket and raked a wisp of hair out of her face. "Is someone bullying you, John?" she said. The furrows in her brow deepened as she looked at him.

"No!" Manjiro said. "No bully."

"Well," she said. "I think you should have a talk with Mr. Whitfield."

"It's nothing," he said. "Just joke."

Mrs. Whitfield cocked her head and regarded him with one raised eyebrow. "Well, if there's trouble, you should talk to Mr. Whitfield."

"No trouble!" Manjiro said.

It was getting late, so Terry and Job said their good-byes. Manjiro went into the cool barn to consider what to do. He didn't think about Japan very often, but once in a while something would happen that would remind him of home. That day when he swung open the door of the barn, the sweet, grassy smell of hay jolted in him the memory of kneeling on the *tatami* floor of the temple. He had a sudden longing to be there—to be at that temple—and to be home.

He went straight to Duffy, who was standing in her stall, swishing her tail contemplatively. She was one of his best friends in the world, and the only one he could speak to in Japanese. She would listen patiently, blinking her huge, dark eyes as if she understood his every word.

He pressed his face against her warm neck and spoke to her of all his thoughts. He told her that he didn't want to get into trouble, but he didn't want to endure Tom's taunts anymore, either.

"Duffy," he said, "what should I do?"

21

FALL DOWN SEVEN TIMES

"A horse race?" Terry cried. "You agreed to a horse race?"

"A horse race? When?" Job said, panting a little as he ran up to join Terry and Manjiro on their way to school.

"In two weeks," Manjiro answered. "Me against Tom."

"Couldn't you have come up with some other idea?" Job grumbled, kicking at a stone.

"I thought it would be fun," Manjiro said.

"Tom's been riding since he could crawl," Job said. "You're not going to get as good as he is in two weeks!"

"And anyway, his dad has the fastest horse in the county!" Terry added.

"Duffy is a farm horse—she's not fast!" Job said. "She's really just a pony."

"How are you ever going to stay on your horse for a whole race, much less win it?" Terry moaned. "You've got a lot to learn, John Mung. And the first thing is how to stay on the horse. Your riding lessons start after school today."

During school, Manjiro tried not to think about the race and to concentrate on his work. But as the days went on, that became harder and harder, partly because of a girl, a girl with glossy chestnut hair and stormy, sea-colored eyes. He had met Catherine on that first day of school, and though boys and girls went to separate classes, Manjiro would see her in the halls and sometimes their eyes would meet. When that happened, Manjiro's heart filled, like a sail fills with wind. Then he would have to glance away or down at his shoes to catch his breath.

He had hoped the horse race would just be a challenge between Tom and him, with a few friends as witnesses. But word got out and it seemed the whole school was planning to attend the event—maybe even Catherine. The possibility of humiliation began to rub at Manjiro like a burr under his shirt.

He started to hope something would stop the race from happening. Maybe some kind of disaster.

"Are there ever earthquakes here?" he asked Captain Whitfield as they lugged bags of feed to the barn.

"No," the captain said. "Not here."

"Not ever?"

"Not ever," he answered. "Why do you ask?"

"I just wonder," Manjiro said.

Maybe someone would break a leg or something. Even if it had to be him, that would be all right—just as long as he didn't have to race Tom Higgins.

Meanwhile, the training went on, every day after school. But no matter how much coaching, advice, and cajoling Manjiro got, he could not seem to stay on the horse for very long.

"Run!" Terry shouted and swatted Duffy's hindquarters with a willow switch. Duffy jumped forward, skittered sideways a little, and then took off at a dead run. Manjiro hunkered down with his head close to her neck, his hand wrapped around her mane, and his knees squeezing her sides.

Terry went by as a sort of smear of color. Then Job, a blur, then everything went by in a blur, until he recognized the approaching splotch of red as the barn, looming closer and closer. And closer. Now the features of the barn stood out, even the knotholes in the siding. He pulled back on the reins, but Duffy was running so fast, so fast! She didn't slow down! She didn't change her gait. What she did was stop. Abruptly.

Manjiro flew up and over her head, mercifully landing in a heap of strewn hay, somersaulted, and sat up. He laughed.

The other boys did not think it was funny. "You keep falling off!" they cried.

"Fall down seven times, get up eight," Manjiro said. "So my mother used to say."

22

THE RACE

There were no earthquakes. There were no broken legs. There were no emergencies of any kind. The day of the race arrived, as days generally did on the farm, with the barnyard rooster incessantly announcing its arrival.

Manjiro climbed out of bed like an old man. Today was the day of his humiliation.

Captain Whitfield squinted up at him from his coffee when he came into the dining room. "Rough night?" he asked.

Manjiro shook his head, trying not to let his gloom show. He had taken great pains to keep this contest secret from Captain Whitfield. He poured himself a cup of coffee, muttering to himself, "I'm not going to let the cat jump in the bag now."

"Pardon me?" the captain said.

Manjiro shook his head and sipped his coffee, the bitterness of it like a rebuke. His relationship with Captain Whitfield had been changing. Now that Manjiro was growing up—he was seventeen now—he regarded the captain more as a friend than a father. There were times, though, like now, when the feeling of being the naughty child of a possibly disapproving father was overwhelming. He should have confided in Captain Whitfield; the captain might have been able to help him out of his predicament. Well, it was too late now. He chewed his bread and jam without tasting it, while the captain's squinting eye burned a hole in him.

"Look here, John," Captain Whitfield began. "I can see that something's been troubling you."

Oh oh, Manjiro thought, he must know about the race.

"And I wonder if maybe you've heard something, and so I think I should tell you myself."

What? Manjiro wondered. What did Captain Whitfield have to tell him?

The captain cleared his throat. "The farm is operating well," he said, "and you have been doing a fine job with your studies."

Manjiro waited. Clearly that wasn't all he had to say.

"The hired hands are doing well, wouldn't you agree?"

Manjiro agreed that they were.

"Mrs. Whitfield has some help now, too," he added. He stood up and looked out the window, then turned back and began again. "Now, listen, John, it would be well for you to learn a trade. I have secured an apprenticeship for you with Mr. Hussey."

"The cooper—the barrel maker?" Manjiro said slowly. So . . . Captain Whitfield had found out about the race, knew that Manjiro had made trouble, and now he would have to stop going to school altogether.

"Not right away," Captain Whitfield said. "Not until next spring."

"Oh . . . ," Manjiro said, "so I keep going to school until then?"

Captain Whitfield chuckled. "Don't look so alarmed! You'll finish at Bartlett. You can keep going to school while learning the trade."

Manjiro heaved a sigh of relief and decided to make a clean breast of it and tell Captain Whitfield everything.

But the captain wasn't finished. "I know . . . ," he began, then hesitated. "I know that you will not stay with us forever. I want to know that you can always make a living—and cooperage is an honest trade. There will always be a need for coopers, I expect."

Manjiro nodded. Captain Whitfield stood up and paced around the table. He *still* hadn't finished, Manjiro realized. What was it he wanted to say?

"Now, here's the other thing. . . ." He paused, then blurted out, "I've accepted the offer to be master of the *William and Eliza*, departing in some few months."

"Oh!" Manjiro was so surprised, he didn't know what else

to say. That was something he hadn't expected at all—Captain Whitfield going back to sea. Of course he would—why wouldn't he? He loved the sea.

"The farm is doing well enough, but it doesn't really pay all the bills!" Captain Whitfield said, laughing. "And what with . . . well . . ." He trailed off.

Manjiro didn't dare open his mouth. He was feeling such a mix of relief, melancholy, dread, and excitement, too, that he couldn't have put two coherent words together. All the feelings condensed into one strange, strong longing that he couldn't put words to, either. He missed life on board a ship. However hard it was, however bad or meager the food, however fierce the storms blew, there was the salt spray, the wind in your hair, the dark night, the stars glittering overhead, the foaming waves, the lovely sound of the ship "talking," and the feeling of both owning the world and being but a tiny speck upon it at the same time. He missed all that, and in a way he longed for it. Most of all, he knew, he would miss the captain, his friend. Finally, that was all he could say.

"I'll miss you," he said.

Captain Whitfield's eyes twinkled in the lamplight. "Ah," he said. "You'll soon have someone else to keep you company."

By the time Manjiro arrived for the race, a large crowd of boys and girls had already gathered along the country road.

Someone was passing out cones of sweetened shaved ice—for a nickel apiece—and dozens of little handmade pennants fluttered in the air.

Tom rode up on a lean and well-muscled horse, several hands bigger than Duffy. The horse pranced and sashayed to the "oohs" and "aahs" of the crowd.

"Look at Tom," Job said. "Look at that black eye. He's been fighting again!"

Manjiro's head was so full of everything Captain Whitfield had said, he barely noticed.

Someone in the crowd yelled, "Nice horse, Tom."

Tom acknowledged this by pulling back on the reins to make the big muscled horse prance.

"What's his name?" someone called.

"That's Lightning!" several voices shouted. "He's famous!"

"Nice shiner, Tom," someone else yelled.

"You should see the other fellow!" Tom shouted. He dismounted and led his horse over to the start area. Manjiro watched as he gently stroked Lightning's legs and checked his hooves, speaking to him in a soft voice.

Tom glanced at Manjiro out of the corner of his black eye. He hawked and spat in the dust near Manjiro's feet and said, "Hope for a miracle."

Manjiro's mouth was too dry to answer.

Job and Terry stood nearby, coaching him: "Remember to squeeze with your knees." "Hunker down." "Hang on." "Don't look around to see where Tom is—never mind about that."

"Just try not to fall off for once!" Job said.

Then it was time. The boys brought their mounts to the starting line. Lightning zigzagged back and forth across the line while Duffy stood placidly behind it, unmoving.

"Hold your horses!" shouted Roger, the self-appointed starting official. The crowd laughed.

Tom reined in Lightning. Duffy casually twisted her head around to nip at a fly on her flank.

Roger reminded the riders that the race course would follow the dirt road to the fence line, then follow the wagon path through the fallow field, which wound back to the dirt road, to finish at the start line.

"On your marks!" Roger said.

The two competitors jammed their feet into the stirrups.

"Get set!"

The boys crouched low in the saddles, leaned forward over the withers, their mouths as close to their horses' ears as they could manage.

The shout of "Go!" set the horses running. Even Duffy seemed to get the message and burst across the start line, dancing a bit before charging off.

Manjiro tried to think of nothing but his coaches' advice. He kept his head down and didn't look around to see where Tom might be.

The crowd's cheers receded behind him, and soon all he heard was Duffy's thudding hooves, her hard breath, and his own short exhalations as he jounced up and down on her back—something he knew he wasn't supposed to be doing.

Now he was alone and he could finally think. He ran through everything Captain Whitfield had said. He was going back to the sea. Manjiro would be starting an apprenticeship. And what else had the captain said—that soon Manjiro would have someone else to keep him company? Who could that be?

He felt sad and a little lost to think the man who had been his one constant friend in all that had happened for the last three years would be leaving. Manjiro supposed that was why Captain Whitfield had arranged for him to learn a trade, so he could be truly independent.

"In—de—pen—dent!" he shouted at the top of his lungs. What *was* this feeling? This out-in-the-open, wind-in-the-hair, whooping-and-hollering, rip-roaring feeling? It was something he'd felt often in America, this land of whoopers and hollerers, of people who laughed whenever they felt like it, sang as they strolled down the country roads, and whistled inside the house, if so moved. They went here and there, traveling to faraway places in fast-moving machines, and nobody troubled them about who they were or where they were going or what business they had in that place. This feeling, he realized as the road raced beneath him, and the bright green spring forest rushed by, and the sky was a moving ocean of blue—this was the feeling of freedom.

What are your hopes and dreams? Captain Whitfield had once asked. A person *could* have ambitions for the future in this country. There was room for hopes and dreams, and he was going to put his mind to it. Right now, Manjiro's hope was that he would win. It seemed possible. Duffy was going so fast, he couldn't imagine anything could outrun her. And he had not fallen off—so far.

He was still in the saddle as he crossed the finish line; then he sprang off Duffy to wave in victory to the crowd. Nothing could have run faster than Duffy—no horse alive. Therefore, he must have won.

But then he saw Tom standing next to Lightning. Had they never started? he wondered. But no, of course, his heart sank when he realized that they had started, raced, and won. And that was why Tom was proudly waving to the crowd.

Manjiro and Duffy were greeted with a smattering of polite applause, a few whistles, and a couple of catcalls. Terry and Job were there. They held Duffy while Manjiro slid off her back, none too gracefully. Manjiro looked at the crowd. Was Catherine there? he wondered, his eyes flickering over the faces. But as he was looking, he noticed that everyone had become silent. And then, when the crowd turned their heads in unison, Manjiro turned to look, too. A big, red-faced man stalked toward them, his hands at his sides balled into tight fists.

"Blast you!" the man shouted, his eyes settling on Tom. "What do you think you're doing?"

The crowd grew ever more still.

Tom answered in a low voice, "I . . . we're . . . it's just a little fun. It's nothing. Really."

"Did I say you could take Lightning?" the man shouted. "*Did* I?"

"Pa." Tom tried to keep his voice calm, the way you'd talk to a dog with bared teeth. "I tried to ask you last night. . . ." His father walloped him across the face.

The crowd took in its breath in one collective gasp.

Tom's father took hold of Lightning's bridle with one hand and Tom's collar with the other and led them away, one on each side of him. He aimed a stream of curses at Tom and every so often delivered a kick to his backside. Every time another kick or blow was administered, Tom hopped or cringed, his swagger gone.

The crowd broke up, with people walking home in small groups, talking quietly. Manjiro and his friends stood around not knowing what to say to one another. Manjiro caught sight of Catherine out of the corner of his eye, leaving with a group of her friends. He would have liked to talk to her, although he didn't know what he could have said. She glanced at him and gave a little wave. He waved back, and then she was gone.

Manjiro walked Duffy back toward the farm, clucking and humming a bit to her, sometimes talking a little to her in Japanese, which it seemed to him she liked, and thinking. There was so much to think about! He reviewed all the things Captain Whitfield had said this morning, but he couldn't help thinking about the race, too, and how strangely everything had turned out.

It was odd that Tom was so gentle with his horse, he thought, yet could be so mean to people. He supposed, too, that although everyone had thought the black and blue marks he always wore had come from fighting, they probably were given to him by his own father. "It seems we didn't really know Tom at all," he said to Duffy, then stopped.

"Tom!" Manjiro exclaimed. "What are you doing there?"

Tom sat in the ditch, his dusty face streaked with blood and tears. He glanced up at Manjiro, his expression transforming from a pout to a scowl.

"I fell," he said. "So what?"

"Fall down seven times," Manjiro said, reaching out to give him a hand, "get up eight."

23

LOVE

Before he left, Captain Whitfield placed both hands on Manjiro's shoulders and said, "You are the man of the house now." Manjiro took it to heart, attending to the farm with earnest effort.

At first, everything had seemed hollow, quiet, empty. Manjiro missed hearing the captain whistling as he strolled from barn to house, and his large laugh—nothing polite about it—ringing out from one of the fields. Mostly, he missed their evening talks on the porch.

And then he discovered *The New American Practical Navigator*, and from the moment he read the title page, he was hooked.

All the secrets of navigation were here, and if he could understand them, he would possess knowledge that no one else in his country yet possessed. "The epitome of navigation!" the title page proclaimed. "All the tables necessary . . . in determining the latitude and the longitude by lunar observation and keeping a complete reckoning at sea!" Holding this book

THE

NEW AMERICAN PRACTICAL NAVIGATOR:

BEING AN

EPITOME OF NAVIGATION,

CONTAINING

ALL THE TABLES

NECESSARY TO BE USED WITH THE NAUTICAL ALMANAC IN

DETERMINING THE LATITUDE AND THE LONGITUDE

BY LUNAR OBSERVATIONS,

AND KEEPING A COMPLETE RECKONING AT SEA;

ILLUSTRATED BY PROPER RULES AND EXAMPLES:

THE WHOLE EXEMPLIFIED IN A JOURNAL KEPT FROM BOSTON TO MADEIRA, IN WHICH

ALL THE RULES OF NAVIGATION ARE INTRODUCED;

ALSO,

THE DEMONSTRATION OF THE USUAL RULES OF TRIGONOMETRY; PROBLEMS IN MENSURATION, SURVEYING, AND GAUGING.

WITH AN APPENDIX,

CONTAINING METHODS OF CALCULATING ECLIPSES OF THE SUN AND MOON, AND OCCULTATIONS OF THE FIXED STARS; RULES FOR FINDING THE LONGITUDE OF A PLACE BY OBSERVATIONS OF ECLIPSES, OCCULTATIONS, AND TRANSITS OF THE MOON'S LIMB OVER THE MERIDIAN; ALSO, A NEW METHOD FOR FINDING THE LATITUDE BY TWO ALTITUDES.

BY NATHANIEL BOWDITCH, LL. D.,

Fellow of the Royal Societies of London, Edinburgh, and Dublin; of the Astronomical Society in London; of the American Philosophical Society, held at Philadelphia; of the American Academy of Arts and Sciences; of the Connecticut Academy of Arts and Sciences; of the Literary and Philosophical Society of New-York; Corresponding Member of the Royal Societies of Berlin, Palermo, &c.,—and, since his decease, continued by his son,

J. INGERSOLL BOWDITCH.

THIRTY-FOURTH NEW STEREOTYPE EDITION.

NEW-YORK:

PUBLISHED BY E. & G. W. BLUNT, PROPRIETORS,

No. 179 WATER STREET, CORNER OF BURLING SLIP.

1865.

in his hands made Manjiro feel like he had discovered a treasure; he felt like the most powerful man on earth.

His desire fueled an interest in earning enough money to purchase his own copy. The odd jobs he did—running errands, painting fences, cleaning chicken coops, splitting wood, and filling wood boxes—kept him so busy, he didn't have time to think of being lonely.

And then William Henry, the Whitfields' first child, was born.

The first time Manjiro bent his head to kiss William Henry on his fuzzy head, he inhaled a smell so sweet and familiar, it made him ache inside.

He was suddenly inside his family's hut in Japan, holding his baby sister—years and years before, right after his father had died. He heard the leaves scraping the thatched roof, the swish of his mother's garment, and the soft sound of her crying, while in his arms, the baby cooed. He inhaled the sweet, grassy smell of the woven mats on the floor, upon which sunlight lay in bright, trembling squares.

Manjiro could gaze and gaze at William Henry and never grow weary of it. And no matter where Manjiro was in a room, the baby's eyes would drift there and rest on his face. He had beautiful eyes, a liquid blue—the color of the sea.

"I used to be afraid of blue eyes," Manjiro whispered to William. "But how could anyone be afraid of you?"

The baby gazed up at him, his face like a polished jewel.

"Someday, when you are grown, you will come and visit me in Japan," Manjiro said. "You will be the captain of a big, three-masted barque and you will sail proudly into Urado Bay. You will walk the road to my home and no one will run away, afraid you are a devil. Everyone will greet you as my brother." Even though he knew it was impossible, still the thought sent a little shiver of excitement down his spine.

Manjiro had to admit: He was smitten with a baby.

That wasn't all. There was also a girl.

24
THE MAY BASKET

The evening of April 30, Manjiro worked at composing a poem. The next day was May Day. The custom was to fill a little basket with flowers along with a handwritten note, then drop it at the door of a girl whom you liked. Upon hearing your knock at the door, she was supposed to chase and catch you and—most unbelievably—kiss you!

"Is she really going to chase me?" he asked Terry.

"Yes, of course, that's the whole point!" Terry said.

Manjiro chewed on his pen, scratched out line after line, and started over for what seemed the one hundredth time.

"What should I say?" he said.

"What do you like about her?" Terry said.

"I . . . just like her!"

"Is she pretty?"

"Oh yes!" Manjiro said. "Very beautiful."

"Then compare her to the most beautiful thing you can think of," Terry said.

Manjiro thought a moment and then wrote that she was as beautiful as a right whale. He read it to Terry.

Terry screwed up his face. "I'm not sure she would like to be compared to a whale."

No, Manjiro thought, he supposed she wouldn't. He struck that out. "A stormy sea is a beautiful sight."

"Forget about beauty," Terry groaned. "What else can you say about her?"

"She has the nicest smell in all the world. She smells as good as rice cooking."

"Yuck!" Terry said. "Who wants to smell like that?"

Manjiro sighed. No one could understand how, when he had smelled rice cooking after starving for five months, he had thought it was the most heavenly smell in the world. "I guess she doesn't really smell like rice," he said.

"Write about her beautiful voice," Terry said. "Does she have a beautiful voice?"

"Yes, of course," Manjiro said. Her voice was like . . . He tried to think of the loveliest sound he knew. "In a stiff wind the ship timbers groan and creak."

Terry laughed. "I don't think you're in love with this girl. I think you're in love with ships and whales and the sea. Listen, don't write about her at all, just make up a little rhyme: 'Roses are red, violets are blue; I hope you will catch me so I can kiss you.' How's that?" Terry asked. "I'm going home to write that, right now!"

After Terry had gone, Manjiro stayed up late into the night, thinking. Not just about Catherine and the rhyme he would have to write. What Terry had said had started him thinking about ships and whales and the sea.

Light was showing at the edges of the horizon when Manjiro finally wrote his poem:

'Tis in the chilly night

a basket you've got hung.

Get up, strike a light!

And see me run

But no take chase me.

He crept out of the house onto the dew-wet grass. Birds were just waking as his feet crunched along the gravel path. He would have to take a shortcut through the fields to reach Catherine's house before she left for school.

He arrived at her doorstep rumpled and muddy. His heart pounded nearly as hard as it had the day his whaleboat was taken on a Nantucket sleigh ride.

He hesitated. He could neglect to knock and walk casually away. If he knocked, he would have to run, for what if Catherine came to the door? She would have to chase him, and if she caught him, she was supposed to kiss him.

He felt himself flush. He wouldn't mind that, but what if

she didn't *want* to kiss him? That would put her in an awkward spot. Perhaps he had better not knock.

And yet . . . it was the custom to knock, then run away—"but not too fast!" Terry had told him. "Or otherwise Catherine can't catch you."

To have a girl catch you and kiss you—right out in public—it made his palms sweat just to think of it.

"Courage," he told himself, and set the May basket on the step. First wiping his damp palms on his pants, he raised his hand again to knock. Just then, he heard voices in the house and he bolted, hopped a fence, and dashed over a hill out of sight.

That day all the young people went "a-Maying" in the woods and meadows, where wildflowers bloomed in profusion. The girls gathered violets and daisies and wove them into crowns and necklaces. The boys mostly broke off small tree branches which they used to whack one another.

Manjiro was walking through the woods on his own when he heard girls' voices in the clearing ahead, and he stopped. One of the voices was Catherine's. Of course it wasn't anything like ship timbers groaning; it was a beautiful liquid sound, much more like—

"I got a May basket from John." Catherine's voice stopped him from finishing his thought.

"John Baker?" said a different voice.

"No . . ."

"John Freeman?" another voice offered.

"No . . ."

"Who then?"

"John Mung!" she said and laughed. It was a beautiful laugh, Manjiro thought, like the song of birds.

"What did you do? Did you chase him?" said a girl's voice.

Manjiro leaned forward. He wondered, too. He had been so nervous that he had not looked back.

"No! I didn't even see him!"

"How did you know it was him, then?"

"Don't you always know when John Mung has been somewhere? There's a little crackle in the air, like lightning is about to strike—like *something* is about to happen."

"Why didn't you chase him?"

"I should have," she said, "I wish I had."

"Really?"

"Well . . . ," Catherine said, "he's such a nice boy."

Manjiro's heart melted like warm butter.

"Maybe he wants to *marry* you!" said a young voice.

They all laughed again.

Well, what would be so funny about that? Manjiro wondered.

"What if he really did? What would you do?" one of the girls asked Catherine.

"Well, maybe I would!"

"Catherine! You can't mean it!"

"Why wouldn't I? Why shouldn't I? He's as fine a boy as any, and smarter, too," she said.

Manjiro wanted to rush out of the trees and kiss her, he loved her so.

"How can you say such a thing?" one of the girls said. "Your parents would never allow it. Think what people would say!"

Manjiro's face flushed. His heart rose into his throat. How could he have been so foolish? How could he have thought he was one of these people? That he could be an American?

Before anyone saw him, he rushed away and ran to his favorite place: a high rock overlooking the sea.

He should have known he'd never really fit in. Goemon had been right when he said he'd never be accepted. When the Whitfields had had to change churches not once, but twice, he should have known. When Tom said he didn't belong in their school, he should have known. Americans had their blind spots, and Manjiro had been blind himself not to see it.

He sat for a time, staring out at that churning green sea,

as tumultuous as his feelings. He began to see all the ways Americans were not so wonderful. They could be greedy; they thought a lot about amassing wealth. Some of them kept slaves! Not the people in New Bedford and Fairhaven, but lots of Americans had slaves. And even those who didn't keep them seemed to think that black-skinned people were not as good as they were.

Manjiro tossed little pebbles off the rock into the sea and laughed ruefully. Americans and the Japanese, when you boiled it down, were more alike than they would ever admit. They both thought they were better than other people—and each thought they were better than the other!

It actually made him laugh out loud, the idea of explaining at home that barbarian girls thought they were too good for a Japanese boy. But he wouldn't be able to explain it, because at home, nobody knew what a real Westerner was like—they could only picture goblins with horns and fangs and enormous noses like bulbous roots growing out of their faces.

He wished he dared to run through the town of Fairhaven shaking people and saying, "Ha ha! You Americans think you are better than the Japanese! But the Japanese believe *they* are better than *you*!"

As he stared out at the sea, he thought of all the times he had stood on the shore or at the stern rail of the *John Howland* wondering, What lies there, far across the oceans? Now he knew at least some of the answer. Did he regret it? No, of course not—he would never regret it. The door through which he had glimpsed such wondrous light, he had walked through. He had encountered both beauty and pain. Now he understood that was how it would always be—no matter where he went in the world.

A wave crashed against the rock and flung cold spray into his face as if to wake him up. He had been in a long dream, but his enchantment had come to an end.

25

THE COOPER'S

His enchantment may have been over, but his work had just begun. Manjiro moved to Mr. Hussey's shop in New Bedford to begin his apprenticeship. He attended school and worked at the shop, and should have been too busy to feel homesick, but he wasn't. He longed for Mrs. Whitfield's warm, fresh-baked bread and thick jam. He yearned to hear William Henry's happy babble and to be able to chat with Captain Whitfield again. At the same time, he began to be homesick for Japan: He missed the foods of his old country; he missed his mother; he even found himself missing things he didn't think he liked! He felt torn about where, exactly, he wanted to be. He just knew it wasn't Mr. Hussey's!

At first he liked the sweet-sharp smell of the freshly cut wood and the way the sawdust shimmered in the shafts of sunlight that filtered through the cracks in the shop walls. But fall came and then winter, and those same cracks let in the wind and the cold rains and the snow. The cooper didn't—or couldn't—feed Manjiro and the other apprentice enough, so they were always hungry. Soon, they both were ill more often than they were well. Manjiro began to feel he would never be warm again; he would always be hungry, and he would always be sick.

In future years, Manjiro would remember little of the cooper's shop except the dreams of fevered sleep. He dreamed once he was sitting outside his family's hut in Japan, untangling a net. The ground beneath him was warm, the sun flickered through the pine boughs. His mother came to the door, but he couldn't see her face—it was concealed in shadow. With a gust of wind the branches blew about, casting slashing splotches of sun and shade. He strained to see his mother's face—he moved his head this way and that, trying to get a better view, but she stayed always in the shadow.

Then he was in a ship on the sea, the wind howling and the boat heeled to one side. The halyards clattered against the masts and the rig groaned against the strain of the wind.

He blinked open his eyes. Was he aboard a ship? He turned to gaze out a frost-rimed window, which rattled and shook in the wind. The world outside was a sea of foaming white snowdrifts.

"Too much sail . . . ," he murmured.

"Perhaps you'd like to climb up the chimney and reef them?" said a voice.

He looked up to see Mrs. Whitfield standing over him, her blue eyes like tranquil pools. Then she smiled and her face crinkled up so that her eyes almost disappeared.

"Don't you worry," she said. "We've brought you home. You're home now, John."

But he still felt a very long way from home.

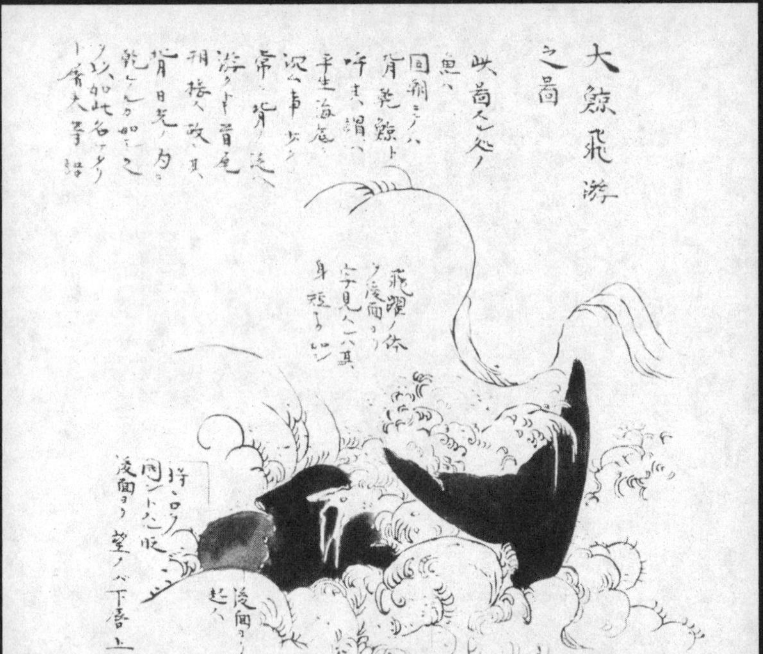

Drawing of a whale

PART FOUR
RETURNING

It is good for young people to experience a good share of hardship or misfortune. A person whose spirit collapses in the face of misfortune is of no use.

—from *Hagakure: The Book of the Samurai*

26

THE FRANKLIN

Late summer 1846 (3rd Year of Koka, Year of the Horse)

Mr. Davis!" Manjiro exclaimed when Ira Davis appeared one day at the Whitfield farm.

"I'll state my business straightaway," Mr. Davis said after Manjiro invited him in and they were seated in the parlor.

Davis had been made captain of the *Franklin,* and he wondered if Manjiro would be interested in signing on as a member of the crew. "You were solid and reliable on the *John Howland,*" he said, "and game to try anything. Remember when we went for the ambergris?"

"I thought you were crazy!" Manjiro laughed.

Davis didn't laugh. His face flushed and he looked down at his hands.

"I'm honored to be asked, of course," Manjiro said quickly, "but Captain Whitfield is gone now, and the farm needs tending. . . ."

"Your friend Isachaar Aken—you called him Itchy, as I

recall—he'll be serving aboard the *Franklin*, too, as first mate," Davis said.

"That's appropriate," Manjiro mused. "*Ichi* means 'one' in my language. Now he'll be 'number one mate.'"

"Just so," Davis said. "Will you sign on?"

"Are you offering me a position as cooper?"

Davis twisted his cap in his hands. "A steward," he said.

"Steward!" Manjiro exclaimed. "But that's . . . I've graduated from Bartlett. And although I haven't finished my apprenticeship, I'm quite capable at cooperage."

"Aye," Davis said. "That's all well and good, but ye're really very nearly a green hand."

"Green hand! I served nearly two years aboard the *John Howland*. You know it yourself."

Davis wagged his head noncommittally.

"Well," Manjiro said, "I don't know how Captain Whitfield would feel about me leaving just Mrs. Whitfield to manage the farm. We have help now, but even so, it's a lot of work."

"There are others who you knew on the *John Howland* who will be sailing with us . . . ," Davis continued.

Baby William toddled into the room, and Manjiro swept him up and plunked him on his lap. "There's also young William here." He kissed the top of the baby's head. "He needs looking after, so I'm afraid . . ."

"We'll be sailing in Japanese waters . . . ," Davis said.

Manjiro looked up. "Oh?"

Davis nodded. "There might be a chance for you to go home."

Manjiro waited a long minute before replying, keenly aware of the toddler's soft grip on his forefingers. "Let me talk to Mrs. Whitfield and I'll give you an answer tomorrow."

When Davis had gone, Manjiro carried William Henry to the window and stared out across the meadow toward the sea. He thought of Captain Whitfield's question: *What are your hopes and dreams?* He remembered Mrs. Whitfield asking him, *Are you going to help the world change?*

"Maybe, baby William," he said, "you will come to visit me in Japan, after all."

Although she was saddened to see him go, Mrs. Whitfield agreed that he *should* go. It was an opportunity for him, she said, and she understood his longing to see his family again—how could she not understand that desire?

Finally, on a brisk and breezy October day, with the sky as blue as baby William's eyes, Manjiro had said good-bye to her, to young William, to Job, and to Terry.

"Only a steward?" Terry had said, but Manjiro just laughed.

"What do I care if I sign on as a lowly steward? I'll never collect my lay, anyway. I am going home!"

Now on board the *Franklin,* he waved to Job and Terry, Mrs. Whitfield and William Henry. He was sad, yes, but he was so excited! Everything—everything!—the roll of the ship under his feet, the fresh breeze off the ocean, even the shouts of the orders—everything seemed to speak of going home.

"Home! Home! Home!" the sea gulls squawked overhead.

Even the timbers groaned, "Going ho-o-o-me."

And, as the ship cast off, the whoosh of water under the hull said, "Ho-o-o-ome!"

"Skip aloft and loose the main topgallant, Mung," came the order. Manjiro grasped the lowest deadeye and swung himself up onto the ratlines.

He had been swept away from Japan when he was fourteen years old. He had been gone for the years of the Ox, Tiger, Hare, Dragon, and Snake—five Western years. Now, in the 3rd Year of Koka, the Year of the Horse, at nineteen years old, he was at last headed toward home.

He started up the ratlines, continued past the main yard, leaning out backward to climb the futtock shrouds, past the topsails, all the way to the topgallant yard. His feet danced along the footropes, one arm hooked over the yard to keep himself from falling a hundred feet onto the deck.

Up here he was like a bird, high on a perch. He gazed out at the tidy houses climbing the hillside, the colorful shops, and the cobbled streets. Tucked in among them were the Stone House School, the Bartlett School, the cooper's shop, and somewhere, up over that hill, was Catherine's house and, beyond that, the Whitfields' farm.

He would never live so privileged a life again, he didn't suppose. Not in Japan. He would never live in such a grand house, or have so much land to roam, or his own horse to ride. His life here had been a fairy tale—the story of a poor fisherboy being swept off to an enchanted world, a life he could not have imagined in his wildest dreams. But he would give it all up to touch the ground of his homeland with his feet, breathe its scent, and be in the presence of his family and his mother once again.

"Laying on!" came a call from the mast, alerting him to a sailor about to step on the footropes. "Dreamin' shan't unfurl the sail," growled the mate who'd joined him.

Manjiro took one look at his shipmate and felt his limbs turn to pudding.

The man's back was not so broad, nor his shoulders so powerful as Manjiro remembered; his golden curls were flecked with silver. But still, Manjiro was sure, it was Jolly.

Jolly didn't look up but simply barked, "Spring to it, man!"

Manjiro glanced down. First the deck was beneath him, then the mast swung over the sea. Then the deck. Then the sea. His insides sloshed from side to side. The men on the deck were like so many beetles; the harbor waves like doily lace.

"What be the matter with ye, mister?" Jolly growled, turning toward Manjiro.

Jolly's face was ruined, his skin creased and scarred. His right eye was pulled off center so that it stared pathetically at the sea. His good eye flickered over Manjiro then back to the yard. Before that fateful night when Manjiro set him on fire, Jolly had not been a bad-looking man—except, of course, for his perpetual scowl. Now his countenance could give children nightmares.

"Ye look familiar," Jolly said, "but I don't see as well as I did. Who ye be?"

Manjiro hesitated. He cleared his throat. "Have you tried spectacles?" he said, in his deepest voice and best English.

"Ach," Jolly growled, continuing to work on releasing the sail. "Specs wouldn't help this crooked eye. It won't see straight with or without glass in front of it."

"Ah." Manjiro hoped Jolly would not ask his name again.

"Mung!" somebody hollered from the main yard.

"Mung?" Jolly said. "I used to know a Mung." Jolly fixed his one good eye on Manjiro's face.

A long, tense moment passed as the two men regarded each other. Jolly's steady eye made a slow sweep the length and breadth of Manjiro. It was obvious to both of them that they were more evenly matched than the last time they'd met.

Manjiro had youthful strength and agility on his side. He could reach out and knock Jolly off the yard. Possibly.

Jolly had years of experience on his side. He could reach out and knock Manjiro off the yard. Possibly.

For one tense moment, the question was, who was going to try first?

Shouts from below indicated that the captain wanted the sail loosed and smartly! Jolly and Manjiro pounced on the work.

Once finished, Manjiro scrambled down the rigging to the deck. As fast as he scurried, Jolly scrambled just as fast, and Manjiro was out of breath when his feet finally touched the deck.

Manjiro tensed to fight, but when Jolly stepped on the deck, he sniffed, hitched up his pants, and said, "We're not too far out for ye to disembark. Fer yer own good, I'd recommend it." Then he strode away.

Manjiro stared after him for a long moment. His threat did not have menace in it, and it was almost as if Jolly were warning him of something—or someone—else.

27

WHISTLING UP A WIND

August 1847 (4th Year of Kokoa, Year of the Sheep)

Manjiro was where he was supposed to be: high in the rig. He was looking where he was supposed to be looking: out to sea. But he was supposed to be watching for whales, and he was not.

He would have liked to be alone, but he wasn't. Daniel, a young green hand, was up there with him, his husky voice pounding Manjiro with questions. "What am I supposed to be looking for?" (Whales.) "What kind of whales?" (Any kind.) "How will I know if I see any?" (Spouts.) "What do I do if I see any?" (Tell me first—just to make sure.) "But how do I know that you won't take credit for it if I see whales and tell you first? Then you'll get the silver dollar instead of me." (Fine, tell everyone, but then you'll feel stupid when it's a false alarm and the whaleboats are already lowered and manned. Trust me, I've done it.)

"All right," Daniel said, "I'll do as you say. But how am I

Drawing of three sailors at the ship's stern

supposed to see whales first if you're here? I mean, you'll spot them and I'll never get credit."

"Listen, Daniel, I'll let you in on a secret."

"A secret? What secret?"

"I'm not looking for whales. So if there are any, you'll see them first."

"What are you looking for?"

"I'm looking for land."

"What land?"

"My country."

"What's that?"

"Japan."

"Oooh," Daniel said, "I hear that place is very dangerous." He drew a finger across his throat. "If you land there, they eat you."

"No, they don't eat people."

"That's what I heard."

"Don't believe everything you hear—especially on this ship," Manjiro said.

It had been a hard voyage. What there was of food had been infested with weevils; the crew was surly and unfriendly, and they had hardly even seen whales, much less caught any. Except for his old friend Itch—now, because he was first mate, respectfully called Mr. Aken—Manjiro had grown used to being shunned. Small groups of gathered men, whether telling stories or singing chanteys, would fall suddenly quiet when he approached. Although he and Jolly had avoided a confrontation, Jolly was generally surly. Captain Davis didn't make the voyage any easier; he was prone to fits of temper.

Manjiro could hear him scolding someone below.

"Lucky we're way up here, out of the way of the captain, eh, Mr. Mung? They say he's 'wet as a scrubber,' whatever that means."

Davis did have a temper, Manjiro thought, but was he really daft?

"The others say you're friendly with him—you were friends aboard the *John Howland.*"

"We were . . . ," Manjiro said.

"Do you think it's true what else they say? That we can't catch whales because there's a Jonah on board? What's a Jonah, anyway?"

"A Jonah," Manjiro said, "is a person who brings bad luck to a ship." He wondered who the crew considered a Jonah and was about to ask when he was interrupted by a shout and an outburst from below. Had someone sighted whales while both he and Daniel were asleep on the job? He swept his eyes over the sea, looking for a spout or flukes, and then saw the dark streaks in the water. Schools of fish, just below the surface.

"Bonito!" came the cry.

Manjiro handed Daniel the wigwag, the whale pointer. "You're on your own now," he said. "I'll go down and lend a hand. I used to be a fisherman, somewhere close to here as a matter of fact." Daniel stayed aloft while Manjiro hurried down the ratlines.

Whaleboats were lowered and crews of whale men turned into fishermen. It was a relief to have work to do, and Manjiro kept his hands busy and his head down. Years ago, the day he and his friends had found the school of mackerel before the storm, the boats had filled with glistening fish, just as they did now.

A shout roused him from his memory. "Mung!" Daniel called down from the topgallant. He pointed the wigwag toward the open sea. Following the pointer, Manjiro caught a glimpse of something there, then nothing. He stopped for a moment to let his eye wander back to that spot.

"Your glass, Mr. Aken?" he asked, and Itch passed him his telescope.

There! Something bobbing on the water. A boat. No, a row of boats, pretty as a string of pearls. His heart leaped.

"Japanese?" Itch asked.

Manjiro's mouth went dry. "Yes, I think so," he croaked.

"Well, heave to, man!" Itch said. "Let's row over and have a gam with them."

First, Manjiro wanted to gather a few things. Back on board the *Franklin*, his hands shook as he tied on his old tunic—once rough and stiff, now worn so thin you could practically see through it. He tied his cloth belt around his middle and grabbed his ragged *tenugui*—his headband. After gathering some biscuits from the galley, he dashed to the deck and opened his mouth to call out. He couldn't help thinking what he didn't dare speak out loud: Home. He was going home.

"What will I say?" he called down to Itch, waiting in the whaleboat below. "I haven't spoken Japanese in years, except to Duffy. Did you know that horses understand Japanese?"

"Never mind all that. Come on. Get in. Let's go!"

Manjiro climbed down into the boat and fidgeted with his *tenugui*. He was more nervous than any of the times he'd gone after whales. His heart whacked away at his ribs so hard they ached.

As the whaleboat pulled away from the ship, he began to imagine the dramatic hills of the coastline, the sound of the boat scraping along the sand, voices speaking Japanese, the smell of fish smoking over wood fires, the rain drumming on thatched roofs, the gentle sounds of his village, and the sight of his family, their faces glowing with surprise and delight at seeing him. His mouth watered at the thought of the nice thick slab of bean jelly they would fix for him to welcome him home.

The splash of oars from the fishermen's boats made him turn his head. They were preparing to row away.

"No!" The word charged out of his mouth. He began again, in Japanese. "Please," he said, "be so kind—wait a moment?"

One boat lingered while the others rowed away. Aken and Manjiro approached the boat, but the fishermen's faces had become like masks.

"They look worried," Itch whispered.

"They are," Manjiro said. "Seeing you is like seeing a goblin. Maybe I seem like one, too." He realized now that it would be hard to trust a person dressed like a beggar, yet who rode aboard a mighty ship, who consorted with foreign devils and spoke in a foreign tongue. "Don't worry," he said, more to himself perhaps than to Itch. "I'm sure it will be all right once I speak with them."

The fishermen kept their oars in the water, but waited until his boat reached theirs. They took the offered biscuits and in turn offered him some of their catch of bonito.

"Thank you. That is kind," he said in Japanese, "but we have caught plenty." The words came out of his mouth sounding stiff and rusty.

They stared at him blankly and gestured for him to take some fish.

"No, thank you very much," he said again, "we don't need any fish."

They spoke among themselves, and Manjiro felt a surge of panic when he realized that he could not understand what they were saying. Their dialect was too different from his own. Perhaps they lived far from his village. Even he had spoken a different dialect from Denzo and the other fishermen, and they only lived a few villages apart.

There were a moment of silence, when all Manjiro could hear were waves lapping at the side of the boat and the achingly familiar sound of straw sandals scraping the wood bottom as the fishermen shuffled their feet.

Surely they could understand something, Manjiro thought, and he said slowly and clearly in his best Japanese, "Can you take me with you?"

They withdrew, visibly shifting their weight away from him.

It was too much to ask them to take him with them. They were afraid, and rightly so—their lives would be endangered—he saw that now.

"Perhaps you can take a message," he said, "a message for my mother?" He dug in his trouser pocket for his letter. Sounds of surprise from the fishermen made him remember his own amazement the first time he'd seen pockets.

He held the letter out toward them, but they stared at the envelope like it might contain poison.

"It's just a simple message," he said, "for my mother. It only says one thing: 'I am alive.'"

He held the envelope out again, but no one reached to take it. In fact, every hand on the boat disappeared.

"I'm sorry, I'm sorry. Please . . ."

He knew they would not take the message. Already, they were hoisting the sail, manning the tiller, stowing the oars.

And then they sailed away. Away toward the low, dark islands he could imagine in his mind's eye, the islands he knew as home, taking his heart with them.

28

A MOMENT

"Mung!" Captain Davis glowered down at him. "Trying to desert the *Franklin*?"

"No, sir! I . . . we . . . ," Manjiro stammered. "You promised that if we got close enough I could make a try for home. Don't you remember? Let me have a whaleboat, Captain." He glanced over his shoulder at the receding fishing fleet. If only he could go now, so he could follow them! "I can row from here," he begged.

"I can't spare a whaleboat. You should know that," Davis said.

"Send a crew with me then, to bring the boat back."

"What? Endanger my crew? Where would I be without a crew? Do you expect me to sail this vessel without a crew?"

"Just a few mates, sir."

"Blood and thunder, *no*!" Captain Davis turned away, cursing. "Trying to steal one of my fine cedar whaleboats! And with white cedar plank up a full three percent!" he yelled, bringing his walking stick down with a *crack* on the decking. "If you want to go to China, ye can swim there!" Davis stomped away, whacking his walking stick against everything he passed, so the deckhands leaped out of his way. "By jiminy, if you try that again, you'll be punished for desertion! You hear me?"

29

THE SEA TURTLE

February 1848 (1st Year of Kaei, Year of the Monkey)

Another year passed. Whale sightings were few, and most whale hunts unsuccessful. The crew was already surly and the captain restless. Then the wind died. The sea was like an enormous silver platter; hot sunlight glinted mercilessly off it. Days and days passed without a breath of wind, and the vessel sat unmoving, its sails hanging listlessly.

The crew was as listless as the sails. A sailor pushed a wet mop about halfheartedly, in a futile effort to cool the decking. Two others slowly carved away at some whalebone, trying to create in their scrimshaw the excitement they lacked on board. Several tended the blisters they'd earned after the rowing they'd done the day before. The captain had insisted they try to tow the *Franklin* out of the doldrums. After they'd been rowing for hours in the blazing sun, blisters rose on their hands and backs.

Small clumps of men cast sullen glances at Manjiro as he passed. A group whispering near the bulwark was suddenly silent as he walked by. Manjiro had become accustomed to this and had ceased to care. Ever since the day he had tried to speak to the Japanese fishermen, he didn't care about anything.

He leaned against the mainmast and stared out at the sea, trying to remember what had motivated him before. As if through a gauzy cloth, he remembered that he had desperately wanted to go home. But now he knew that would never happen.

It didn't matter anyway, Manjiro told himself. He wouldn't be accepted at home anymore. Better to live out his days in the middle of this endless, motionless sea. If they didn't make landfall soon, there might not be many of those days left anyway. The little water they had was brackish and foul, the pork moldy, and the biscuits more weevil than bread. Some of the men were suffering from scurvy.

A sharp voice punctured the quiet. "No wind yet? No whales, neither, I suppose."

Manjiro identified the voice as the captain's, speaking to the sailors on the quarterdeck. He couldn't see Captain Davis, and since he was hidden by the mast, neither could the captain see him.

The crew was silent. No one wanted to cross Captain Davis. He'd started out with tongue-lashings, moved on to lashings with the "cat," and had now taken to stalking about the deck waving a musket.

"I know there's the superstitious among ye. Don't think that I don't know there's talk of a Jonah aboard."

Was it the captain the crew thought was the Jonah? Or—Manjiro swallowed hard—was *he* the one they blamed for their bad luck?

"Is it you, stripe pants?" Captain Davis spoke to Wilcox. "You, eye patch?" That to Grimley. "Nay, I think ye all know who the Jonah is, don't ye? Where is he? The time is come to tend to it."

Manjiro held his breath. The crew knew where he was. Would they do what he'd heard they did to Jonahs—would they throw him overboard?

"If none of ye lubbers will fetch him, I'll start pitching ye into the sea, one by one. Who should I start with? One's as worthless as another. Here's the old, half-blind man—who'd miss him? Here's just a child, worthless, too—a green hand!"

When he heard Daniel squeak as if squeezed, Manjiro flew out from behind the mast. A long moment passed as the sullen faces of the crew regarded him, and he them. He looked at the angry, twisted face of the captain, who had once been his friend. Daniel's frightened face pleaded to Manjiro from under Davis's arm.

"There he is," Davis said. "He knows himself where the fault lies—take hold of him!"

A shout from the port side of the ship distracted everyone. The captain dropped Daniel, who darted away, and the crew scurried to the bulwark to look. Something floated on the surface of the water. Like a large shadow, a giant sea turtle drifted into view. Manjiro felt a chill race through him when this creature from the watery depths turned its dark eye on him.

"Fresh meat!" hollered one of the mates.

"Catch it!" a sailor cried.

"Kill it!" shouted another.

Someone snatched a knife out of another man's hands and flung it at the creature, with cries of protest from the owner of the knife. The knife struck the turtle's head, slicing into its hide, then glanced off and was lost to the sea. Blood oozed from the wound, staining the water purple.

"Lower a boat!"

"A net!"

"Harpoons!"

The turtle paddled in an uneven circle, then dove.

Manjiro watched for a moment, then pulled a short knife from his belt, kicked off his shoes, and in one powerful bound leaped up onto the rail, over the side, and into the water.

Down, down he plunged into the murky green sea, his knife slicing the water ahead of him. Bubbles and a wispy trail of blood rose like smoke from the descending turtle. Manjiro followed it down.

When his hand struck the leathery shell, he curled his fingers around a flipper. He felt himself jerked and pulled by the beast, and was surprised at its strength and speed. Everything seemed to fall away from him as he raced through the brilliant shades of blue and green. Bubbles percolated along his skin, cool as ice.

He had saved the captain the trouble of throwing him into the sea by doing it himself. But he wasn't just sinking—he and the turtle were going somewhere with great purpose, hurtling toward something. Time fell away; there were just the two of them and the silence.

When he was young, Manjiro's mother had told him the story of Urashima Taro. Taro was a poor fisherman who rescued a turtle from some mean boys who were tormenting it. The turtle rewarded Taro by taking him away to an enchanted world under the sea.

He could hear his mother's voice telling the story of this boy and the princess he loved in the undersea kingdom. The princess wore a dress of shimmering pink shells, each one twinkling like a star, with glittering jewels woven into her hair.

"Twenty maids attended her, each in a dazzling dress of abalone and pearl," his mother's voice said in his ear. "In the palace a banquet table was laden with . . . Why are you listening to this silly story, child? You'll drown if you don't let go and swim up!"

Can't . . . , Manjiro thought. Turtle is taking me to that place. . . .

"You know how the story turns out. Taro lives the life of a prince, but what does he end up wanting more than anything?"

To go home, Manjiro thought. To go home to see his old parents. Taro wanted this so badly that he left the beautiful princess and the glittering kingdom for it. Manjiro did not need to go to the undersea kingdom to know that was what he wanted, too—more than anything else.

He would swim up, Manjiro decided. He would swim up, breathe, and live. He would find a way to go home. He would find his old friends, and they would all go home together.

All of this, yes. But first, the turtle. How many times on Bird Island had he looked longingly at the sea turtles floating on the sea? Only once in five long moons had Manjiro managed to kill a turtle, and then it had been a small one.

He groped for the head. His fingers found the ropey neck, and he brought the knife across the turtle's throat in one swift movement.

He would recite a sutra for the turtle later. Right now, he needed air. Urgently. Desperately.

Gripping the turtle's flipper, Manjiro began to swim up. Up and up he kicked, towing the heavy carcass behind him. His lungs about to burst, he knew he had to breathe. If there was no air to be had, it would have to be a breath of water, but breathe he must.

Above him, the sunlight pierced the murky gloom of the water, and he lunged toward it.

A rush, and then a roaring sound. Air surrounded him the way water had a moment ago, and he took great, gulping mouthfuls of it. When he glanced up at the ship, he saw his mates stamping their feet on the decking and yelling. No, not yelling—cheering! And laughing. Even Jolly was smiling. The captain, however, was not. He glared down at Manjiro before turning sharply away.

30

SAILING CLOSE TO THE WIND

Sometime during the night, Manjiro woke. Something was different. At first he couldn't put his finger on what it was. But when he heard the whoosh of the water moving under the hull, the insistent ticking of the halyards, and the straining of sails filled with wind, he knew: The ship was moving!

Manjiro slid into his trousers and went above deck. A glorious wind pushed at his hair and billowed his shirt. Sea and sky were velvety, the night embroidered with a million glittering stars, every wave frosted with silver moonlight.

It seemed as if everyone on board had turned out. The wind had blown their foul mood away, and as he passed they clapped him on the back, shook his hand, offered a kind word.

It was all very strange. Why were they suddenly friendly, and why so quiet? The men practically tiptoed about on deck.

Jolly was standing near the tryworks, his crazily crooked eyes twinkling in the lamplight. A small group of men huddled around him, whispering. Manjiro recognized

Gridley and Dunn and the blacksmith Lafayette among them. Nothing so unusual about it, except the intensity of their conversation.

They glanced at him and he moved away, assuming they would only scowl.

"Mung!" Dunn called out quietly.

"Over here." Gridley waved him over.

Manjiro moved toward the cluster of men.

"'Twas brave what you done today," said Dunn. "Going after that sea turtle like that."

"You turned our luck—see, now we got wind!" said Gridley.

Daniel padded up to them, panting. "Captain's in his quarters," he whispered. "Maybe we should lock him in!"

"A poorer idea I never did hear," Jolly said, whisking Daniel's cap off his head and whacking him with it, "for where do ye think the firearms are stowed? Let's stick with the plan."

"Jolly has a plan," Daniel said.

Jolly whacked him again. "I just said that, didn't I?"

"He ain't got any plan," Lafayette said.

"Who says I don't?" Jolly snapped, then whispered to Manjiro, "We aim to take control of this vessel."

"That's . . . mutiny!" Manjiro said.

"Shh!"

"Mutiny is a serious business." Manjiro lowered his voice to a whisper. "They can hang you for it."

"Don't you think we know that?" Jolly said. "But you can see for yourself how it is! I tried to warn you about Davis that first day, but you were stubborn and stayed aboard, didn't you?"

"You were warning me about *Davis?*" Manjiro said.

"Of course!" Jolly said. "Who did you think I meant?"

"You!" Manjiro said. "I thought you were threatening me."

"Pah!" Jolly spat. "You're worried about *me,* when the captain goes around in his underclothes, ranting at the clouds, threatening his crew with a musket?"

"Cap'n's going to kill somebody one of these days—count on it!" Gridley added.

"Does Mr. Aken know about this?" Manjiro asked.

There was a pause, and then Jolly said, "We aren't sure about him. You, neither, tell you the truth. You being friends with Davis on the *John Howland* and all."

Manjiro wondered for a moment if this could be an elaborate plot to get him into trouble. "What's your plan?" he had begun to say when a loud blast interrupted him.

They turned toward the sound to see the captain appearing to float along the quarterdeck in his white nightshirt, musket in hand.

"A ghostly apparition," Lafayette whispered.

Davis paused to reload, muttering and shouting by turns, "Ye'll find whales, *ye* lazy louts, or *ye* shall feel the bite of the musket ball!"

He paced along the deck, raving and waving the gun. When he came to the tryworks, he turned his back for a moment and Manjiro's shipmates seized the opportunity to dive behind a whaleboat. Manjiro turned back to see Davis glaring down at him.

"Don't think I don't know what you're up to," he said.

Manjiro felt sweat trickle down his back.

"You're planning to steal one of my whaleboats!" the captain said.

"No, sir!" Manjiro protested, relieved at least that the captain didn't seem to know about the mutiny. "Even if I was, we've left the islands of Japan far behind. They're too far away now for a boat to do me any good."

"So you admit you plan to steal a boat?"

"No, sir! I only meant . . ."

"Go ahead, take a boat," the captain said. "Lower a boat now!"

Manjiro paused.

"Spring to it, man!" Captain Davis shouted. "Why don't ye jump?!" He slammed the butt of his musket down on the deck. "Lower away!"

For a moment Manjiro dropped his eyes, unsure of what to do. He couldn't disobey a direct order! But if he obeyed, would Davis really insist Manjiro cast off? Here? Alone? In the dark and the wind and hundreds of miles from anywhere?

Manjiro looked up when he heard the hammer of the musket being drawn back. Davis had hoisted the gun to his shoulder and sighted down the barrel—at Manjiro.

31

THE HARPOONER

After an initial rush of fear, Manjiro realized he was shaking, not with fear, but with anger. He told himself not to get angry, but he *was*. Davis had never intended to let him go home to Japan. It had been a ruse to get him to sign on—for a steward's lay.

What would Captain Whitfield do in this situation? Manjiro wondered. He did get angry at his crew sometimes, and he let them know he was angry, but he kept his temper under control.

"Mr. Davis!" Manjiro said sharply, as he imagined Captain Whitfield might say it. Davis jumped a little—Manjiro had surprised him. Even so, Davis managed to keep his gun leveled at him.

"Remember your place!" Davis growled, poking the musket barrel at him. "You're a subordinate! You don't talk to your captain that way."

Manjiro's anger boiled up. Anger for every time he'd been treated as someone who didn't deserve a voice, as someone with nothing to say, as someone whose opinion did not count—whether it was because of the family he was born to, because of the way he looked, because of his poor language skills, or because of his lowly rank.

"I'll have my say!" he said firmly.

Davis flinched and took a step backward, and Manjiro moved toward him. "I'll spend three or four years on this vessel, and for what?" Manjiro said, walking deliberately toward Davis. Davis, meanwhile, stepped backward. "I'm an educated navigator, a trained cooper, and I'm doing a full seaman's work on this ship for a steward's lay. You promised me a chance to go home! You did that just to get me to sign on as a steward—for what amounts to no pay—didn't you? What did you promise the others?"

By now Davis had been backed up to the whaleboat behind which Manjiro's shipmates crouched. Manjiro lunged forward and knocked the musket from his hands, and Jolly and the others jumped up from behind him and wrestled him to the ground.

At the same time, a shout rang out from the top of the main mast. "Flukes and spouts!" called the lookout.

There was an eerie pause while they all looked at one another. Were there *really* whales? If there were indeed whales sighted, the captain should call out the orders. But he was in the process of being bound with a hook rope.

"Thar she blows!" cried the lookout.

"Where away?" Jolly shouted up to him.

“Two points on the weatherbow!” came the call.

“How far off?” Jolly called.

“A mile and a quarter” was the answer.

“Set a course to follow through the night,” came a voice outside the circle.

Manjiro spun around. It was Mr. Aken.

“You realize, I hope, the implications of your actions.” Aken stooped and picked up the captain’s musket from the deck.

“Yes, sir,” the men murmured.

“Mutineers might dance at the end of a rope,” Aken said, “if just cause be found.”

The men’s heads drooped.

“However,” Aken continued, “if we can come home with our cargo crammed full of oil barrels and casks filled to the brim with spermaceti, I warrant the owners will be pleased enough to forgive us such transgressions. Especially since it’s as plain as daylight that poor Mr. Davis’s wits are scuppered.”

The men rumbled their agreement.

“Now,” Mr. Aken said, “let’s get to the business of electing new officers. We’ve got whales to catch!”

After Davis had been secured belowdecks, Mr. Aken was voted captain, the second mate was promoted to first mate, and others moved up to fill open positions. Discussion ensued on how to fill the remaining harpooner position. Manjiro's mind drifted as he wondered what the plan for mutiny had been. He did not think the mutiny had gone according to any plan. It had just happened.

"It's important we choose our boat steerers and their crews with care," Mr. Aken was saying, and he went on to remind the crew of their sacred duty to catch whales. "Elsewise, how will our wives and daughters maintain their tiny waists, without whalebone to stiffen their corsets? Think how the horses will loll in the streets, stopping to nap, while those in stalled buggies curse us for not bringing them baleen for buggy whips. Think of unstiffened caps and hats, suspenders, bonnets, ribbons. What of the fishing rods, divining rods, back supporters, tongue scrapers, penholders, boot shanks, shoehorns, and brushes of every description that won't get made without the help of the mighty whale? All the machinery of our modern world would grind to a halt without whale oil for its lubrication. And most of all, consider our friends and neighbors, our families, sitting in the darkness without oil for their lamps!

"A pod of whales awaits us at first light. As you know, we need harpooners with experience and most especially mates we can trust with our lives."

There was silence while everyone thought this over.

Everyone wanted the most reliable, levelheaded, and steady person in a job like this.

"John Mung!" someone shouted.

"Aye! Aye!" a chorus of voices sang out.

"A vote," Captain Aken said.

The vote went all the way around the group with "ayes" from everyone until the last person: Jolly.

He was silent for a moment and then said, "I know John Mung. I was with him the first time he went out on a whale chase, on board the *John Howland*. He didn't understand a word we spoke."

Well, that wasn't entirely true, Manjiro thought.

"And I gave him a wee bit of a hard time, I warrant."

And that was a bit of an understatement, Manjiro thought.

"And I was none too pleased to see him aboard the *Franklin*, truth to tell. But I will admit he has courage, showed when he flung himself into the sea after our supper. And he has nerve, demonstrated tonight in his going toe-to-toe with our former captain. The fact that he can last an entire watch with Danny-boy there," he jerked his thumb to indicate Daniel, "shows he has patience. And he can put up a fight when necessary which I know from . . . personal experience." He paused to scratch at his bad eye. "So I guess my vote is 'aye.'"

The vote was unanimous. Manjiro would be John Mung, harpooner.

32

THE WHALE

Manjiro did not have time to even consider whether he *wanted* to be a harpooner before he found himself standing in the bow of the whaleboat, his knee jammed into the "clumsy cleat," braced to throw a harpoon. He was vaguely aware of the coaxing coming from the headsman in the stern of the boat.

"Pull, lads! Pull like vengeance! That's it, we're gaining! Crack your backbones. Burst your hearts. Burst your liver and your lungs. But pull! Pull, me hearties; pull, me heroes. Don't give up now, blast ye! Lay on, lay on! Are ye awake or asleep?"

Because the rest of the men faced backward to row, only the headsman and Manjiro, who both faced forward, could see what was going on in front of them. Just off the starboard bow, an island seemed to rise out of the ocean. The island grew and grew until it was the size of a continent, a continent with one enormous eye.

"If you could see that whale, mates," the headsman urged, "you'd pull till your eyes popped like buttons."

Manjiro wished they wouldn't pull so hard.

"Softly now! Easy, lads, easy . . . There! There! Harpooner. Stand by your iron."

Manjiro remembered the first time he'd been in a whaleboat, and had turned to see Jolly standing where he stood now. He remembered how repulsed he'd been that these foreigners could kill so cruelly and his fear that they might kill him and his shipmates, too. Now the lance rested in *his* hand. Next to the whale, it seemed no more than one of Mrs. Whitfield's darning needles.

In the distance he could see his shipmates' whaleboats surrounding the shining backs of other whales. Those whales looked like islands, he thought, shuddering at the image of Japan's islands, like a pod of whales, all surrounded by whalers with their killing lances raised.

"Harpooner, stand by your iron," the headsman said, and Manjiro's attention snapped back to his task. The water boiled around them as the beast rose higher and higher.

"Now . . . give it to him!" the headsman called out.

As if on its own, the lance left Manjiro's hand. Everything seemed to stop as the harpoon spun toward the whale, its steel shaft flashing in the sun. He could not pluck it back. What would happen now was inevitable.

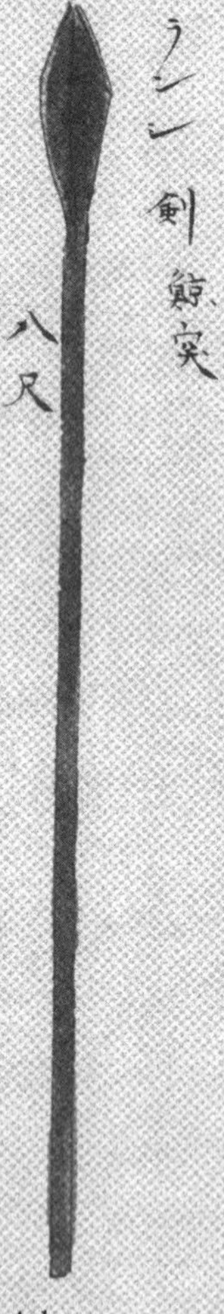

A lance

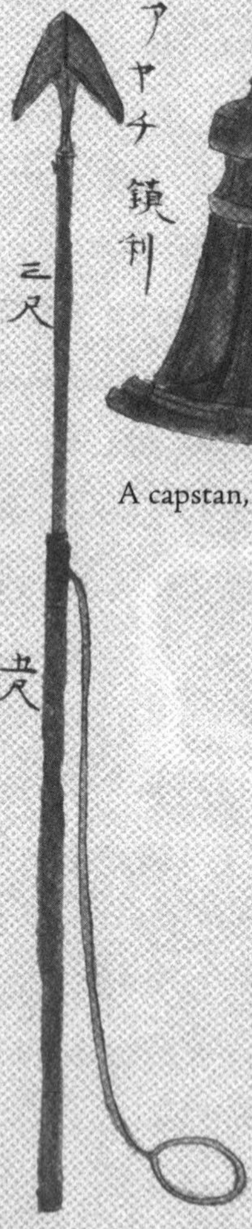

A harpoon

A capstan, which winds rope

The whale's spout would gush blood until the water became thick with it; his blow hole would choke with blood; he would bellow in pain, thrash, and die.

Manjiro knew his whaling days were done. He wanted—needed—to go home.

As the boat pulled its cargo back to the ship, Manjiro pondered on his vision. Would the Western world destroy the country he remembered as home? It would be better if the Japanese welcomed the West, rather than waiting, unknowingly, to be destroyed by them. But how could that ever happen? His countrymen hated and feared the "offal-eating demons" of the Western world. How could they ever welcome them?

Beyond the desire to see his mother, his family, his homeland, Manjiro felt he had another purpose there. He had started to have an idea back in America—he supposed it was a kind of dream. Now, he thought, if he had helped to change Jolly's prejudices, maybe he could do the same in Japan—even if it had to be one person at a time. Maybe he could help change the world.

He would need money—more money than he would make on this whaling voyage. Somehow he would have to find a fortune.

Then he would retrieve his friends from Oahu and go home.

33

TORI

February 1849 (2nd Year of Kaei, Year of the Hen)

Manjiro breathed in the scents and drank in the color of the island. Chattering monkeys scampered up trees. Birds darted among the branches in a blur of red, a flutter of blue, a streak of yellow. After so long on the sea, it was pleasant to dig his feet into the warm sand and listen to the pounding surf—the sound of sea meeting earth.

The *Franklin* would take on fresh food and water here, and some of the mates had been allowed to come ashore and do some shopping of their own. Life on board had improved since Mr. Davis had been handed over to a whaling office in Manila. By now he probably had been sent home on another American vessel.

Islanders rushed to greet the sailors with things to sell: sweet potatoes, breadfruit, coconuts, grass skirts, chickens, and monkeys. A man jogged along leading a pig at the end of a piece of twine. People carried masks made of coconut shells, necklaces made of sharks' teeth, woven mats and baskets, and wooden carvings.

Manjiro studied all these things, hoping to find a gift for William Henry. He counted up the years he'd been gone. Manjiro was now twenty-two, and William Henry would be five years old by the time Manjiro returned to Fairhaven. Young William deserved a very fine gift considering all the missed birthdays and Christmases.

He was pondering what would be the right thing when a voice croaked behind him.

"*Konichiwa?*" the voice said.

Manjiro spun around and looked into the crowd, searching for a face that looked like his. *Konichiwa* meant "hello" in Japanese.

"*Konichiwa?*" he answered. "Hello?"

Where had it come from, this voice? Not from anyone he could see.

"*Konichiwa?*" the mysterious voice said again. Manjiro's eyes darted toward the sound, his gaze drawn up and up until he spied a brightly colored bird perched on the branch of a palm tree: a parrot.

The parrot studied Manjiro with one glittering eye, then winked. Manjiro winked back. He was quite sure he had found a special new friend for William Henry.

Manjiro bargained with the owner of the bird, who had purchased it from someone, he said, who "look like *you!*" Maybe another shipwrecked Japanese sailor. He had met a few in his travels—all trying to find a way home. Manjiro didn't know of any who had succeeded.

Manjiro hurried to the *Franklin,* anxious to introduce the parrot to his shipmates. But when he arrived, the ship was abuzz with exciting news: "Gold! There's gold in California. Loads of it! They say there are chunks as big as slush buckets littering the ground. All you have to do is get there and pick it up!"

On the long voyage home, Manjiro mulled over this news. He would go, he decided. He would go to California and use the gold he found there to get himself and his old friends back to Japan.

In the meantime he set in to teach his parrot, Tori (which meant "bird" in Japanese), more Japanese words. Since she already knew *konichiwa* ("hello"), he taught her "good-bye" (*sayonara*). Then "thank you" (*arigato gozaimus*) and "sorry" (*gomen nasai*). That way, William Henry would know some words when he came to visit Manjiro in Japan.

By the time they reached New Bedford, Manjiro was quite proud of the bird's extensive vocabulary. He couldn't wait to see William Henry's eyes light up when he saw the gift.

* * *

Everyone aboard the *Franklin* was on edge as she sailed into the harbor on a fine September day. Surely news of their mutiny would have reached New Bedford. How would it have been received? Would they have heard the mutineers' side of the story? It was unclear whether their letters would have reached home before other versions of the episode may have been told.

So when Manjiro saw Captain and Mrs. Whitfield waiting at the pier when the *Franklin* made port, he was nervous. He also remembered that he had signed on without the captain's permission. Would the captain be angry? These feelings were mixed with the excitement of seeing his good friend, whom he hadn't seen for five years.

With Tori perched on his shoulder, Manjiro approached the Whitfields slowly.

"No need to worry, John," Captain Whitfield said. "We heard what happened and everyone understands the circumstances."

Relieved, Manjiro smiled and hugged Mrs. Whitfield and clasped hands with his old friend. "I am sorry for leaving without speaking to you," he said.

"You needn't be!" Captain Whitfield said. "I am proud of you for taking the initiative to sign on to a whale ship. I heard you were even promoted." He nodded to the bird perched on Manjiro's shoulder. "And you've made another friend," he said.

"Aye, that I have, but I intend Tori to be a friend to young William." He looked around for the boy. "Where is he? Is he in school? Does he do well with his studies? Or is he helping with the harvest? I'll wager he's as strong as any farmhand there is. . . ." Manjiro paused, noticing Captain Whitfield's bowed head. His friend had aged. Flecks of white shimmered in his hair, and his forehead was creased with lines. Mrs. Whitfield looked worn and tired, too.

"Alas, John, I feared you wouldn't have gotten the news," Mrs. Whitfield said. "William Henry was stricken with fever and died some time ago."

A sudden wind came up, and Manjiro felt it blow right through him. He looked up at the hills of the town, ablaze with their momentary burst of autumn color. The most beautiful things of this earth are the most fleeting, he knew. This knowledge was no comfort now. What was the world without William Henry? The brightness had gone out of it.

"I bought this bird for William Henry, to teach him Japanese. So when he came to visit me in Japan . . ." Manjiro couldn't finish his thought.

Tori scooted down his shoulder and tapped his head sympathetically.

"Hello, Henry?" the bird said. "*Konichiwa?*"

• • •

In the days that followed, Manjiro rarely left the house. He watched as Tori flapped aimlessly from one heavy piece of furniture to the next. She had lost feathers; she looked scruffy and thin. It pained him even to look at her. What had he done? He had taken this beautiful bird away from the sunshine and warm ocean breezes and brought her to live out her long life in a dusty parlor. Instead of flitting from one coconut palm to another, she flapped about in autumn gloom.

The bird made him feel something he usually didn't: sorry for himself. He, too, had been torn away from his home by forces beyond his control and made to live in a foreign and sometimes hostile environment.

But what was to be done about it?

34

THE DAGUERREOTYPE

October 1849, Fairhaven

Manjiro stood leaning on his spade, listening to the wind in the trees. It'd be a fine sailing day. With the wind astern, a bark like the *Franklin* could probably clip along at ten or eleven knots and put a hundred miles between it and New Bedford by dusk. He shook himself free of such thoughts. It would not be right to leave the Whitfields now—he was needed here. He tried to turn his mind back to digging potatoes.

"Mung!" Terry ran up and stopped to catch his breath. "Come along with me."

"I can't. I'm working," Manjiro said.

"No, you're not," Terry said. "I saw you. You were dreaming. Now, come along. The portrait man is here and I aim to get my portrait made."

"The what man?"

Terry took his arm and marched him down the road,

chattering about the daguerreotype man. "He makes likenesses of people by way of a new kind of invention called the daguerreotype," he said. "Sometimes they call it 'photography.'"

Just outside of town they came upon a brightly painted wagon, where a man was trying to set up a sign that had blown over. When it was upright again, Manjiro read, PRIVATE AND MOURNING PORTRAITS. 25 CENTS FOR 1/16TH PLATE. Samples of the photographer's work were on display, and Manjiro and Terry stared at them in amazement.

"It's wondrous what they do," Terry said breathlessly. "It's so exact, it's almost more real than looking in a mirror. And fast! Not like sitting for days or weeks to have your portrait painted—and who can afford that, anyway?"

While the portrait man got his machine readied, Manjiro stared at the pictures. There were portraits of families, of husbands and wives, and even recently deceased people—so their loved ones had an image of them to keep. Every detail was there and perfect. As Terry had said, it was like looking at a reflection of someone.

"Now, listen, John. I've made up my mind. I'm going to California to try my luck in the gold fields. That's why I'm getting my portrait made. It's for my folks—to remember me by. Who knows how long we'll be gone!" Terry said.

"We?" Manjiro said. "Who's going with you?"

"Why, you, of course! What else are you going to do—make pennies on a whale ship for the rest of your life?"

The photographer had Terry sit on a chair in front of an elaborate backdrop and readied his machine—a box on a tall tripod.

"I don't know, Terry," Manjiro said. "How can I leave the Whitfields now? I can't go and leave them without any family."

"You'll come back! You'll come back *rich*!"

Manjiro shook his head. "No, Terry, if I go, I won't come back. The only reason I wanted to go in the first place was to earn enough money to get myself and my friends in Oahu back to Japan."

"Now, there can't be any talking," the portrait man said. He ducked his head under a black cloth that hung from his boxlike machine.

"You're asking too much!" Manjiro joked to the photographer. "Asking Terry not to talk—it can't be done!"

Terry laughed and the man said, "And no laughing, either!"

Terry stopped laughing and winked, flashing a smile at Manjiro.

"Nor any winking!" The man poked his head out from the cloth and threw up his hands. "And no smiling! Don't you understand? You may not move your body, hands, face, or mouth, or the daguerreotype will be blurred!"

A few moments of silence passed and then Terry whispered, "You're a grown man, John. You must be . . . what? Twenty-two years old? In our country, young men strike out on their own. The captain and his missus wouldn't expect anything else. They'll be having other babies—just you wait and see. No, on second thought, don't wait. Let's go!" He slapped his knee.

The photographer emerged, shaking his finger at Terry. "Listen, young man. I will not abide any more of this. If you continue, the likeness will be nothing but a smear." Then he turned to Manjiro. "If you will promise to keep him silent, I will give you a discount on a daguerreotype of yourself. You can leave it with your loved ones—it will be as if you're still here."

"That's a cracking idea!" Terry exclaimed.

Manjiro did not think a daguerreotype would be the same thing at all, and he declined the offer. Still, he wished he had a likeness of his mother. He turned back to the portraits on display and tried to imagine seeing a portrait of her, tried to bring her face back to his memory, but it was shrouded in shadow, sadness, and longing.

It was time to go home to Japan. His lay on the *Franklin* had only amounted to three hundred and fifty dollars. That would not be enough to get him home. But it might be enough to get him to California.

The photographer came out from under his cloth and shook his head. "I'm finished. I hope the print is not a smear of movement, but if you want to try again, you'll have to pay again."

"No," Terry said, "I'll take it however it turns out."

When they returned for the finished picture later, Manjiro wondered if the daguerreotype would capture Terry's continual expression of surprise. But the photographer had been right—Terry was a blur, as if already on his way.

35

THE GOLD FIELDS

Spring/Summer 1850 (3rd year of Kaei, Year of the Dog)

"The streams are paved with gold, it says here," Terry said. He'd been reading from *The Gold Regions of California* all the way down the coast of South America. Even as their ship tossed and heaved in the enormous seas of Cape Horn, he read. "There are gold veins in California hundreds of miles long and wide. You only have to scratch the surface to uncover the stuff!"

From San Francisco, on board a steamship bound for Sacramento, Terry read from *Three Weeks in the Gold Mines*. "Gold is two times heavier than lead," he recited.

"Imagine that!" Manjiro said. "We're on a vessel powered by steam."

"Gold is nineteen times heavier than water," Terry said.

"See? That big iron wheel powered by steam—instead of wind—that's what makes the ship move."

"Are you listening to me?" Terry said. "I said that gold is nineteen times—"

Drawing of a steamboat

"The speed, Terry! Can you believe the speed?"

In Sacramento they boarded a train, another wonder that Manjiro had never experienced. While Terry tried to describe a thing called a "long tom" used to sluice for gold, Manjiro drew sketches of the train. Then he gazed out the window as the landscape sped by in a blur.

"So many forms of locomotion in the world!" Manjiro said. "When I was a young boy in Japan, I knew of only two: fishing boat and my feet. This is the real treasure, right here: railroads and steamships and square-rigged sailing ships. Fast-moving things. Things that could take me home so swiftly. Isn't it ironic that in order to get home, I have to go dig up the heaviest thing there is?"

"We'll have to watch our budget," Terry said as they bounced along mountain paths on horseback. "One of these fellows told me a jar of pickles and two sweet potatoes cost him eleven dollars!"

And, as they struggled along on foot, up a pass too steep even for horses, Terry continued, "A box of sardines costs sixteen dollars, a pound of bread two dollars, a pound of butter six dollars . . . and who knew it would be such hard work? And we haven't even gotten there yet!"

At their destination, Terry and Manjiro scrambled down a steep bank toward a stream already swarming with gold-seekers.

"Here's a spot!" Manjiro called to Terry.

The riverbanks were littered with pickaxes, pans, and shovels alongside slouchy canvas tents. The air was filled with orders being yelled, shouting, and arguments.

"Whoever left this spot must have struck it rich," Terry said as he and Manjiro waded into the icy-cold water.

"Gave up, brokenhearted, more like," said a grizzled man downstream, caked head to toe in dried mud.

"Remember what I told you," Terry said. "Gold will sink

to the bottom of anything. A river, for instance. That's why it works to sluice or pan for it. See now, let everything else slosh away and see what's left in your pan. What've you got?"

Manjiro gazed at the bottom of his pan. There was dirt and gray pebbles and gritty sand, but also something glittery.

"Gold!" he shouted.

At once there were a dozen men gathered around him, looking down into his pan—and laughing. Laughing and pointing at him.

"Fool's gold!" said one of them.

"And here's a genuine fool along with it!" said another.

"Greenhorn!" they shouted. Laughter echoed up and down the length of the stream.

Manjiro's face flushed. Terry patted him on the back. "Don't worry," he said. "No doubt they did the same thing the first time they saw the stuff." He picked the shiny flakes out of the pan and tossed them back in the river. "See how it floats? There it goes to fool some other soul." He winked at Manjiro. "Remember what I said? Gold is the heaviest thing there is. It sinks."

The other men went back to work.

"Also," Terry said, "gold does not glitter or sparkle. It has a dull luster."

Although Manjiro wanted to climb under a rock in the

river, he put his head down and went back to work. Soon he was lost in the rhythm of scooping the river bottom and sluicing away the dirt, the silt and sand, and the sparkly stuff that was not gold.

Days blended into weeks and weeks into months. Only having lived through those long months on the *Franklin* without ever sighting whales kept Manjiro from becoming discouraged. Scoop, shake, sluice, shake, sluice, stir, sluice . . . became the rhythm of his life.

Other gold-seekers around him gave up. Backbreaking work, bouts of dysentery, standing all day in ice-cold water, and the high cost of living chased many of them away. But more came, and the river was always full of miners.

One day, Manjiro's mind was adrift, far away on a ship at sea, yet his body did the same thing it had been doing for months: scooped up river bottom, shook and sluiced, stirred and sluiced, until all the rocks and sand and grit and pebbles were gone, and there was nothing left at all. And again, scoop.

The day was bright. Terry had staked a claim on another section of the stream. The river was crowded with men standing in the frigid water sluicing and panning, or using cradles or long toms. The clash of shovels and pans, along with splashing, grunting, some idle talk, and a snatch of a song echoed back to Manjiro: "Oh, I come from Sacramento with a washbowl on my knee. . . ."

But for a moment, all the noise faded away until there was just a quiet roar in Manjiro's head. He stared down at the heavy, dull-colored lump that remained in the bottom of his pan after everything else was gone. So this is what dreams look like, he thought. Not shiny and glittery. Just a dully gleaming lump of metal, heavier than water, heavier even than lead.

To Manjiro, this strange, twisted bit of metal meant one thing: He and his friends were going home.

Drawing of Japanese villagers

PART FIVE
HOME

Have your whole heart bent on a single purpose.

—from *Hagakure: The Book of the Samurai*

36

BETWEEN TWO WORLDS

January 1851 (4th year of Kaei, Year of the Boar)

Manjiro heaved with every muscle in his back at the oars of the *Adventurer*, steering, he hoped, toward the islands he couldn't see but knew lay behind him. He imagined the dark shapes appearing and disappearing in every swell of the sea.

Everything had fallen into place, for the most part. From San Francisco he'd gone to Oahu. There he'd found his friends—a joyous reunion—and discussed with them his plan. They'd find an amenable captain to take them, and the whaleboat he'd purchased, on a ship bound for China. They would be dropped off near Japan, and they could row the rest of the way in the boat he'd named the *Adventurer*.

It had all gone according to plan, more or less, except Toraemon wouldn't come along, and Jusuke, Manjiro was sad to learn, had died. But the captain of the *Sarah Boyd* had agreed to take them on as far as the waters off Japan. Now, on the day of their departure from the *Sarah Boyd*, it was storming.

"'Come back to Japan with me,'" Goemon shouted over the wind. "That's what you said. You never said, 'Perish in a storm with me.'"

Manjiro shook the ice out of his hair and pulled on the oars again. He didn't know if he propelled the boat toward land, held it steady, or was merely exhausting himself for nothing. But he pulled again.

"We lived through a storm worse than this one," Denzo said, "or have you forgotten?" Denzo bailed the water that sloshed over the side while Goemon cowered, moaning, in the bottom of the boat.

There had been five of them that day ten years ago. Manjiro remembered clinging with his fingernails to the thwarts of their boat while it tossed in the stormy sea. The wind had howled; hail and sleet had poured from the roiling gray clouds. Just as it did now.

"Toraemon was the smart one, staying in Oahu. Even Jusuke had the good sense to die before having to endure this!" Goemon groaned as another icy wave crashed over them. "Even if we make it through this storm, it'll be only to have our heads chopped off by the shogun. We should have stayed in Oahu"—Goemon gripped the gunnels of the boat—" or at least stayed safe aboard the *Sarah Boyd* instead of getting in this little boat."

Manjiro gritted his teeth to prevent snapping at Goemon. He remembered how seasick Goemon had been on the *John Howland,* how he hated the sea and never wanted to be on it again. He had hated Bird Island, too, because it was surrounded by water.

Another wave curled over the side of the boat.

"There's more sea in the boat than out of it," Goemon said.

"Then bail!" Manjiro tossed Goemon a bucket.

Goemon whimpered as he scooped out icy water. "'I have bought a fine boat that will take us home,' you said. 'If we can just get close enough to the islands, it will get us there.' Another one of your fine ideas. Like going to America. If America was so wonderful, why didn't you stay there, among your friends?"

"Look!" Denzo shouted. "Land!"

Manjiro, facing backward in order to row, could only imagine the jagged rocks and wind-twisted trees, the rounded hills rising from the sea.

"We're really there, aren't we?" Goemon said with growing excitement. "We're really home."

"Home," Manjiro said. He rolled the word around on his tongue as if it were a sweet plum. Home. Would it be home?

Of the ten years he'd been away from Japan, he'd spent almost six of them on the sea. Would life always be like this for him—in a storm-tossed boat, madly trying to steer toward one shore or the other? He had already begun to miss America, just as, when he'd been away, he missed Japan. As the hull of their boat scraped the beach, he knew he would long for his family in America as much as he had longed for his family here.

"I hope you will never forget me," he had written to Captain Whitfield before he left Honolulu, "for I have thought about you day after day; you are my best friend on the earth, besides the great God."

The men jumped out of the boat and dragged it out of the surf. Then they fell to their knees in gratitude.

"Ah—the soft sand of our country," Denzo said.

"And the sweet air," Goemon said, inhaling deeply.

"And the fragrant pines," Manjiro sighed.

"And the . . . ," Goemon paused and the others followed his gaze into the trees. ". . . men who have come to arrest us," he finished.

37

SPIES!

First a face. Then a hand. Then a swish of a robe. Figures appeared in the shadows of the trees.

"Get the gun," Goemon said.

"No," Manjiro said. "It will seem like we intend to hurt them."

"What if they intend to hurt *us*?!"

"If they do, then they will," Manjiro said, "because there are going to be a lot more of them than us."

"What do they have in their hands?" Goemon cried.

They *were* carrying something. Knives? Daggers?

Manjiro laughed. "It's sweet potatoes! They're bringing us food!"

A village of curious onlookers stood timidly at the fringes of the trees, staring at them. A few brave souls approached and offered them steaming sweet potatoes and bowls of rice.

When Denzo showed them his empty flask, the villagers rushed to take it and fill it with water.

"You see, Goemon?" Manjiro said. "These people don't want to harm us."

Manjiro turned back just in time to see the crowd part, all of

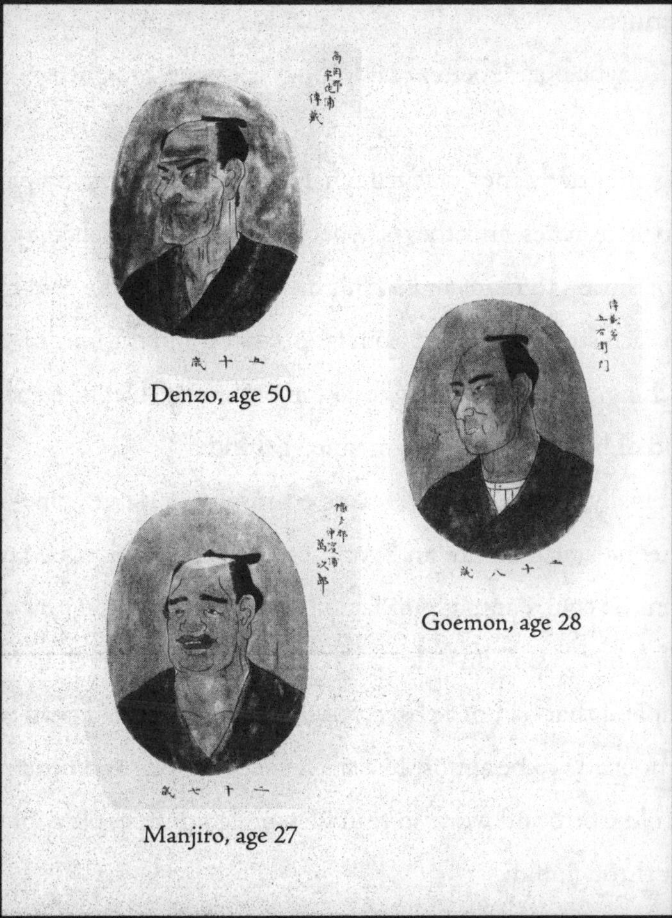

Portraits of the surviving members, in traditional garb, upon returning to Japan

them bowing deeply from the waist. Several official-looking men wearing grave expressions walked through the crowd toward the fishermen.

"Maybe not," Goemon said, "but *these* people might."

Long after dark, they trudged on. The officials who accompanied them lit torches and they staggered forward. Rain had turned the pathways to mud, and Manjiro's feet sank into the cold muck with each step. Exhausted from lack of sleep and the long night of marching, he felt he could not take another step. Denzo struggled ahead of him and Goemon moaned behind.

Finally, the entourage stopped under a large pine tree. Someone started a fire and got a pot of gruel cooking. Manjiro sat on the cold, damp ground and fingered the tattered *tenugui* his mother had given him so long ago. He rubbed the soft cloth of the headband that had once been rough and stiff but had been worn so smooth as to be almost like silk. He felt as torn and tattered as that old cloth, and worn so thin he wondered if people could see right through him.

"What will happen to us?" Denzo whispered. "They say we are spies!"

"Just do as they say," Manjiro mumbled. "Perhaps then they will see we mean no harm, and they will let us go home to our families."

38

THE DAIMYO

Fall 1851 (5th Year of Kaei, Year of the Rat)

Manjiro pushed up the sleeve of his kimono so it wouldn't drag in the ink. He sat on the floor in front of a low table, brush in hand. He was practicing the character for "garden," which, he thought, might as well be the same as the characters for "prison." Since there was so often nothing else to do, he was using the time to learn to read and write his own language.

He paused to stare out at the courtyard. In the small garden, three trees surrounded a tiny pond. In spring, the cherry blossoms had burst into bloom, covering the tree in mounds of pale blossoms. The blossoms fell, the leaves unfurled, and summer came. A humid silence had settled on the garden, broken only by the splash of a frog.

It was a tranquil prison, but it was still a prison.

Many moons had waxed and waned, and they still had not been allowed to see their families, or even to send messages to them. Why had he ever thought he could help bring change to Japan? He could not convince anyone of anything! He was not able even to convince the authorities of his and his friends' innocence and their simple desire to go home.

Officials came and went. Sometimes they wanted to talk to the fishermen. Some wanted just to look at them; some wanted to interrogate them, as if they were spies. Manjiro, Denzo, and Goemon told the story of the shipwreck over and over. They explained that thunderstorms occurred in other parts of the world, not just Japan, and that the Milky Way could be seen everywhere. They were asked to eat with chopsticks, to prove they were Japanese.

Now the courtyard was gray and colorless, shrouded in mist. Manjiro sat at the low table, brush in hand. He was just pushing up the sleeve of his kimono when the officials came and asked for him. Just Manjiro. Alone.

"Manjiro!" Goemon clasped Manjiro's hands in his. "Be careful of what you say. You can't just say anything you like. It's not like America!"

"I'll be careful," Manjiro said.

On the far side of the courtyard, Manjiro was ushered into a large room. Compared to American rooms crowded with tables, chairs, rugs, cupboards, and bric-a-brac, the rooms in Japanese houses—even houses used as prisons such as this—were open, airy, and uncluttered.

Even so, Manjiro found it a little hard to breathe. Across the room a daimyo, Lord Nariakira, sat on his knees on a raised platform. His silk kimono rustled elegantly as he waved to dismiss the other officials in the room. Manjiro immediately sank onto his knees and pressed his forehead to the floor.

"Tell me about this country you have been to—America," the daimyo said.

Manjiro looked up to see the great lord's eyes flash. Was it with interest? Or malevolence? Manjiro knew the way he answered Lord Nariakira's questions could determine his fate. His heart pounded; he heard the familiar roar of fear in his head.

He remembered his determination to change how the Japanese thought of foreigners. But he so desperately wanted to go home to his family. Perhaps if he gave simple answers, they would let him go.

He said, "In America, women put holes in their ears and string thread with beads through the holes." He paused, then went on. "American toilets are placed over holes in the ground. It is customary to read books while using them."

The daimyo's stare was piercing. "Is this all you have to tell me?"

This man would not be impressed with little novelties, Manjiro saw. He wanted to know things. Important things.

So Manjiro said, "America is an open country and learning is constantly becoming greater," he said. "It has made many inventions. Like . . . a telegraph. A telegraph is a wire stretched high above the road, and a letter goes from one station to another without the aid of a messenger."

The daimyo listened quietly.

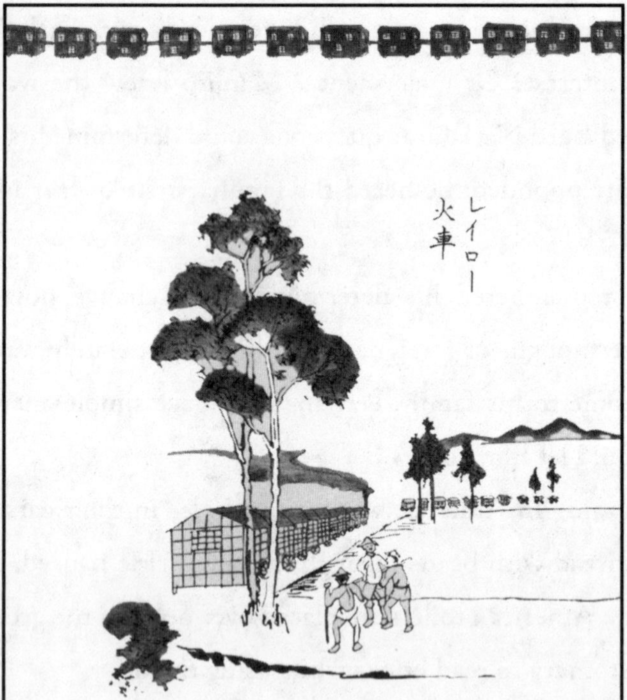

Drawing of a train

"I think the letter is drawn by a magnet iron," Manjiro continued.

"Go on," Lord Nariakira said.

"They have also something called a railroad. It consists of twenty-three or -four iron boxes chained together. The cargo is placed on top and the passengers sit inside. These boxes have two or three windows with glass panes. When one looks through them when the train is in motion, its swiftness is so great that objects are seen only for an instant. This land ship runs on iron rails."

When Lord Nariakira asked about ships, Manjiro talked at length about whaling vessels, how swift they were—and they were not the swiftest! He told of their many sails and how superior they were in weathering storms, and how they could carry thousands of barrels of oil and dozens of men. Westerners, he said, had mastered the art of navigation, and now they built vessels that did not need wind, for they were powered by steam! "In the hold of the vessel they make a fire. Steam is given off from a boiling cauldron, and this turns a motor, which causes wheels on both sides of the ship to revolve. The ship then runs on the sea as fast as flying. This is called a steamship. I can find nothing to compare with it."

The lord offered Manjiro a cup of sake and asked him to

tell him about the American government and the country's military strength.

"The American government is said to be the best in the world," Manjiro said. "There is no hereditary king. Instead, a man of great knowledge and ability is elected king. He sits on the throne for four years. This king is known as the President of the United States. He lives very simply and goes about on horseback, followed by a single retainer. There is no distinction between classes. Even a man of low rank may become an official. Birth and family are of little consequence; individuals earn positions according to their abilities. Respect for personal rights is a basic principle of that society."

He raised his head to glance at his inquisitor. The daimyo nodded thoughtfully, his face placid and serene. "What about weapons?" he said. "Firepower? Guns?"

Manjiro drew a picture of the battlements he had seen in Boston Harbor. "Even the small port of the town where I lived is fortified with guns," he said. "The shells are about ten inches in diameter. The guns measure some twelve feet. Ships are supplied with cannons, and the sailors armed with rifles. There is hardly any weapon that can frighten Americans out of their wits."

Then he quickly added, "But America is working to develop its own country. It has no time to attack other countries."

The daimyo glanced out at the garden. Sunlight had begun to pierce the mist. Then he unrolled a large scroll on the floor in front of him. Manjiro recognized the world map he had brought with him, one of many things that had been confiscated. Manjiro crept forward and gazed at the map, losing himself once again in the cool blue of the oceans. The first time he had seen a map like this, everything had seemed unworldly, impossible, unreachable. Now he had been to many of these places. He knew the white sand beaches on this coast and the mountains that seemed to erupt from these islands. Here there were peacocks, and here snow piled up as high as houses. Here cold winds blew, but here the air was soft as the breath of babies.

"This is the world," he said. "Here is America." He took a deep breath and rushed on. No matter what happened, this might be the only chance he had to have his say. "When a whaleship or a trading vessel is delayed by a storm," he said, pointing to the waters off the coast of Japan, "there is a shortage of water and fuel. The Japanese government drives all vessels away, whether the crew is suffering or not. The Americans would like to get permission to get these things at Japanese ports. Americans do not want to conquer Japan, only to be able to find a harbor here where whalers and other ships may resupply."

Lord Nariakira stood facing the courtyard. He was silent. Manjiro wondered if he had said too much, if he had angered the powerful lord. A gust of wind blew into the room, lifting the edge of the map. "The weather is changing," the daimyo said.

Manjiro nodded. "As is the world," he said.

The lord turned to look at him, one eyebrow raised.

"But I believe good will come out of this changing world," Manjiro said.

39

NAGASAKI

"Nagasaki!" Goemon cried. "But that is even *farther* away from our homes! Why do we have to go there?"

"Lord Nariakira says it is just a formality," Manjiro said. "He has written a letter encouraging our release. I think, after this one last official visit, we will be allowed to go home."

But as soon as they arrived in Nagasaki, they were put in prison. This time the interrogators were not friendly, like Lord Nariakira, but cruel. Every few days they were dragged to a courtyard and forced to kneel in the hot, white sand. The three men were pounded with questions, then dragged from their beds to answer yet more. Manjiro told the interrogators everything he'd told Lord Nariakira and then some.

Finally, exhausted and weary, they were escorted into a courtyard and shown an image engraved on a copper plate. Manjiro recognized the image of the Madonna and child. They were told to stamp on the image. *Fumi-e,* it was called; it meant they had rejected the foreign religion.

"Just do it," Manjiro said, "then they'll have to let us go."

The men stamped on it as instructed.

"Now we will be allowed to go home," Manjiro said.

But instead they were taken to a cell so small it was like a cage, and so low that they couldn't stand up in it.

As they entered, Manjiro heard whispers and scuffling feet, and when his eyes adjusted to the gloom, he saw they were not alone. Several forlorn-looking souls sat along the wall with their knees drawn up to their chests. They were castaways, too.

"What will happen to us?" Goemon said.

"This is just a formality," said one. "They always do this just before they release you."

"So we have heard," grumbled another.

"Have you heard the news?" someone whispered.

"The shogunate is disintegrating," said another in hushed tones.

"Did you know," said a hoarse voice in the far corner, "that China is falling to the West?"

No, they said, they didn't know. They had been so isolated these last many months, they had not heard anything.

"Rival daimyo are trying to grab power from one another," said a prisoner.

"The Dutch have been warning the shogun about the West," said another. "They tell of their guns and firepower, about the might and strength of the West, and that America is like a big, angry giant waiting to attack! Do you know? Is that so?"

Manjiro thought of the ramparts he'd seen in Boston Harbor, and ships bristling with cannons. "America is strong, yes," he said. "It has many weapons. But it isn't angry! America doesn't want to attack Japan!" He hoped he was right.

"It's whispered there will be civil war here. And perhaps war with the West," said the voice in the corner.

Manjiro, Denzo, and Goemon glanced at one another. To what kind of world had they returned? If they survived imprisonment, would they survive the country's turmoil?

40

THE ROAD HOME

June 1852 (5th Year of Kaei, Year of the Rat)

From his resting place on the road that would take him home, Manjiro drank in the air, crystal clear, smelling faintly of salt and feeling very much like freedom. He had walked with his friends to their own hometown, and now he was on his own. They had been given some money, along with most of their belongings, and had been released with the admonishment not to talk about their experiences in the West. Manjiro had talked about it so much these past two years, he felt empty of words.

Shielding his eyes with his hand, he gazed out at the glittering expanse of sea. Except for a few small fishing boats bobbing close to shore, it was as vast, blue, and empty as the sky.

The road, however, was busy. Commoners traveled by foot, carrying bundles on their heads, or rice baskets over their shoulders. Samurai rode on horseback and in *kagos*, platforms carried by their servants. When samurai went by, everyone along the road bowed. When mighty daimyos with their long processions passed by, the commoners dropped to their knees, heedless of dirt or mud, and pressed their foreheads to the ground. Manjiro often had the urge to ignore this custom, but he would be back in prison—or worse—if he did.

At the moment, Manjiro paid no attention to the bustle. His thoughts raced across the water toward distant shores.

An old man had paused at the top of the hill to catch his breath. "What do you see out there?" he said.

Manjiro turned to him and bowed. "Ships, *Ojiisan,*" he said. "Big ships, sailing this way."

The man squinted out at the blue sea. He turned to others passing by. "Do you see ships coming? Big ships? I cannot see them, but perhaps we should alert the authorities!"

Others stopped to peer out at the ocean.

"Nothing," said one.

"Just fishing boats," said another. "What was it you said you saw?"

"Worlds," Manjiro said. "Whole worlds sailing this way."

"Ach," the old man spat, "he is crazy." He moved past Manjiro, waving his arm dismissively.

The others shook their heads and continued on. Manjiro, with two more days of walking ahead of him, struck off toward home.

◆ ◆ ◆

Outside his village, he stopped. He had left the village a fourteen-year-old boy in a ragged tunic and straw sandals and was returning as a grown man dressed in a formal *hakama* and *haori*. What if no one recognized him?

Manjiro's boyhood home, by Masamichi Teraishi, circa 1900

Below him lay his village—the same sleepy village he had left almost twelve years before. Smoke from cooking fires and from the smoking of bonito rose lazily into the sky. When the smell reached him, he almost wept. This was the smell of his village—this mix of salty ocean air, fish, and smoke as sweet as incense.

Things seemed familiar and yet unfamiliar. There was the

town—its cozy houses and narrow streets—nestled between the hills and the ocean. There was the hill on top of which stood the temple and the cemetery. But everything seemed so small compared to how Manjiro remembered it! Everything except the ocean, which, from his vantage point on the hill, seemed to stretch forever.

As he walked down into the town, butterflies danced about him as if to welcome him home. Children he did not recognize swarmed around, asking, "Who are you? Are you the famous man from this village?"

"No, I am not famous," he said.

Finally, he stood before the familiar thatched roof, wooden walls, and bamboo door of his family's hut. On the hard-packed earth next to the house, a wooden bucket sat half-filled with water. A cotton *yukata* hung drying on a pole outside the house. It was as if he had been gone only a few days.

But what would he find when he entered? Would his mother be there? What if the door opened and a completely different family greeted him?

He had thought about this moment for such a long time. He had prepared himself for any possibility as he hiked the road home. But now, as he stood before the door of his family's house, he could barely speak what he had longed to say for so long.

"*Tadaima,*" he said, his voice thick with emotion. "I am home."

Several faces appeared at the door. Not the faces of his brother and sisters, but grown-up people. He could see that they did not recognize him. He hardly recognized them.

But then an older woman stepped out from the shadow of the door and their eyes met. A moment passed between them and he was once again a young boy, standing at the door of this hut, saying good-bye before going to work for Imasu-san.

Without her eyes ever leaving his, she walked to him and touched his face.

"Manjiro," she whispered.

"*Okachan,*" Manjiro said. "Mama."

Later, after neighbors arrived, bringing red sea bream mixed with boiled rice, red beans, warmed sake, and other gifts of food, after his family had taken him to the cemetery to see the stone they had placed there when they thought he was dead, and after much laughter and many tears, Manjiro gave away the few gifts he had been allowed to keep.

He had a mirror for his eldest sister, Seki; buttons for his younger sister, Ume; a pair of dice for Seki's husband, Etsusuke; and a small bag of white sugar for his brother, Kumakichi. He brought needles and scissors and medicines, books and maps.

Finally, Manjiro produced a small box. He took his mother's

hand and poured into it dozens of tiny but perfect shells. It was as if he poured out diamonds, the way the others clustered around, begging to see.

"I wish they were precious stones, but they are only shells," he sighed, "shells that I collected in places where I traveled."

His mother held out her hands to show the shells—small and curved, frilled and ruffled, or smooth as teardrops. They were pink as cats' tongues, shiny brown and speckled, iridescent black, or creamy white.

"*Kirei!*" she said. So beautiful!

Nestled among them was the oyster shell from which he had drunk water on Bird Island. But most were just pretty shells that he liked because, like him, they had washed onto some far shore. No matter where they landed, whether on black sand or white, among pebbles, cobbled rocks, or tossed onto driftwood, still they sparkled and gleamed.

"These shells are like the people of the world, *Okachan,*" Manjiro said, speaking not just to his mother, but to everyone. "They come from many different places. They come in many different colors and sizes. But they are all beautiful."

41

THE SAMURAI

Long after all the others had gone to bed, Manjiro stood at the door of the hut. The moon made a path of light leading to the ocean and beyond—perhaps all the way to America. It looked as if he could walk there on that path of light.

It was so still, he could hear the rush of waves on the beach; the solemn hoot of an owl rolled down the mountainside. Beyond that was a deep and ancient silence, as old as these hills.

It was hard to imagine anything changing this remote village, but the wind of change was blowing, and Japan would be swept along by it one way or another. She, his beloved country, had spent hundreds of years living from full moon to full moon while the West had sped ahead in science, invention, transportation, navigation, and, most ominously, military strength. There were hundreds of ways Japan would benefit from the coming changes. And hundreds of ways she would not.

Perhaps one day even the quiet of this peaceful village would be pierced by the shrill screaming of steam whistles, the chugging of locomotives, the rattle of buggies, the clatter and hubbub of commerce.

But impermanence was the nature of life. Wasn't it funny, Manjiro thought, that his countrymen, who so admired the fleeting beauty of cherry blossoms and the maple's momentary burst of fall color, clung so fervently to the past? They were like the last fragile blossoms that tremble on the branch while the wind tears and tears at them.

Manjiro sighed and went inside, lay down on his futon, and joined his family in sleep.

Manjiro opened an eye to pale gray light and wondered what had awakened him. He heard an unfamiliar voice announce itself as a messenger's.

"The outsider, Manjiro, must go to Kochi without delay," the messenger said.

"Excuse me," said Manjiro's mother, "he is not an outsider; he is just as Japanese as you or I. Why must he go right away?"

"The great lord of Tosa has decreed it, that is why," the man said.

"But what does he want with my Manjiro?" she insisted.

"I'm sure he doesn't tell me!" he said. "I am just a lowly messenger!"

Manjiro's sister offered the man tea and a rice ball, and he became more talkative. "Some people say he is a foreign spy," he said, "so perhaps he will be imprisoned."

Manjiro heard his mother's intake of breath.

"But others say," the messenger continued, "that Lord Yamauchi wants him to teach young samurai the barbarian's language." The man lowered his voice to a whisper. "They even say that he will be made a samurai himself." He clucked his tongue. "Imagine—a simple fisherman becoming a samurai!"

Manjiro smiled, remembering what he had told his companions in the fishing boat when they thought they were going to die—that he wanted to be a samurai. He didn't know why he had said that—it just came out of him. But once he had said it, the idea had taken on a kind of life of its own. Somehow, this impossible idea had helped keep him alive.

The messenger slurped his tea, then chortled. "Well, since he has neither the family nor the upbringing of a samurai, I hope he has the heart of one! He is going to need it."

Within him, Manjiro knew, beat a heart scoured by sand, pounded by waves, burned by sun, and polished by rain and wind. It would always be the simple heart of a fisherman, but perhaps it had also become the mighty heart of a samurai.

EPILOGUE

In July 1853, just months after Manjiro began his teaching career, a fleet of four American ships entered Edo Bay. Commodore Matthew C. Perry demanded to speak to the emperor and made it known that America wanted access to Japanese ports.

Painting of Manjiro, or John Mung, circa 1877

The country was thrown into chaos. "Black dragons belching fire!" the people cried, having never before seen steamships. "One hundred thousand devils" were coming, it was said, and people hid their valuables and locked themselves in their homes.

Suddenly, Manjiro, with his unique firsthand knowledge of America, was needed in Edo, by order of the shogun. He was appointed as a samurai to the shogun, allowed to carry swords and to take a second name. It was unprecedented for a person not born of a samurai family and of such low rank to be elevated to such status.

Although he wasn't allowed to speak directly to the Americans, he argued for an end to Japan's isolationist practices. He reminded the advisors to the shogun that "there are hardly any weapons that will frighten the Americans out of their wits" and that "America is working to develop its own country" and wasn't interested in attacking Japan, but only wanted to get permission to resupply at Japanese ports.

These arguments had an impact. On March 31, 1854, after Perry's second visit, a treaty declared peace and friendship between the United States of America and Japan, ending Japan's 250-year-old isolation policy.

In spite of his service to the shogun (and also because of it), Manjiro lived under a cloud of suspicion for the rest of his life. He was considered by some to be a traitor and by some a foreign spy. His life was in enough danger that he found it necessary to hire a bodyguard to protect him against assassins.

Nonetheless, he went on to achieve many things in his lifetime. He designed ships capable of crossing oceans. He translated Nathaniel Bowditch's *The New American Practical Navigator* into Japanese and wrote the first English book for Japanese people: *A Shortcut to English Conversation*. He taught navigation and shipbuilding, English, and mathematics. He started the whaling industry in Japan and joined the first Japanese embassy to the United States as an interpreter. On the voyage to America, when during a storm the captain of the ship became too seasick to sail, Manjiro took charge. "Old Manjiro was up nearly all night," an American officer wrote in his journal. "He enjoys the life, it reminds him of old times." Nineteen years after leaving America, when he was forty-three years old, Manjiro finally visited Captain and Mrs. Whitfield again as part of a diplomatic delegation to New York.

Manjiro was married three times and was father to three children. In his later life, he could be seen strolling the streets of Tokyo wearing a kimono, Western-style shoes, and a derby hat. Until his death in 1898 at age seventy-one, he began each day with a breakfast of bread and jam and hot, black coffee.

The friendship between Manjiro and the Whitfields lives on in their descendents, who meet at the Japan-America Grassroots Summit held alternatively each year in Japan and the United States. The relationship is also continued by the sister cities of Fairhaven, Massachusetts, and Tosashimizu, Japan, a city near Manjiro's hometown. These relationships continue the work Manjiro began: promoting friendship and understanding between the two nations.

HISTORICAL NOTE

THE BOY WHO DISCOVERED AMERICA

Manjiro told his story to the court of Lord Yamauchi of Tosa in 1852. It was collected by Kawada Shoryo in four volumes called the *Hyoson Kiryaku*.

The Heart of a Samurai is based on the life of a real person, real events, and a real time in history. Fourteen-year-old Manjiro really was shipwrecked along with four fishing companions on Bird Island (Torishima). They were rescued by an American whaling ship, the *John Howland*, and the captain befriended young Manjiro, eventually bringing him back to America with him. Manjiro is believed to be the first Japanese person to set foot in America and has been called "the boy who discovered America."

While living in Fairhaven, Massachusetts, Manjiro attended both the Stone House School and the Bartlett School of Navigation. He was apprenticed for a while to a cooper and also helped out at the Whitfields' farm, where he had his own horse to ride. The Whitfields did, indeed, have to change churches twice before they found a church that fully accepted Manjiro.

After studying in the United States for three years, Manjiro shipped out on the whaling bark the *Franklin*. While aboard the *Franklin*, Manjiro jumped into the sea and killed a sea turtle, earning the respect of the crew. When the captain, Ira Davis, became violent and irrational, he was relieved of his duties by the crew, and Manjiro was promoted to harpooner. On the way home from this voyage, he purchased a parrot in Suriname.

In 1850, Manjiro traveled to California along with hosts of other gold seekers. He managed to find enough gold to finance a trip back to Japan with two of his original companions. No sooner had they landed than they were arrested and held for one and a half years. Finally, they were released to go home to their families. Three days into his visit with his family, Manjiro was called back to the city and given the lowest samurai rank of *sadame-komono*, extraordinary at that time in Japan's history. Shortly thereafter, the American naval commander Commodore Perry arrived in Edo harbor, demanding that Japan open its doors to the West. As an English speaker with firsthand knowledge of America, Manjiro became an advisor to the shogun, who elevated him to an even higher samurai rank. When presented with the *daisho,* the two swords of the samurai, he felt so awkward wearing them that instead he carried them wrapped in a towel.

The things he wishes he could tell his mother in Chapter 17, the letter he refers to in Chapter 36, and the things he says to the daimyo in Chapter 38 are all his words. Many of the characters are based on real people, including Captain Whitfield and his wife, baby William Henry, Manjiro's friends Job and Terry, and his four fishing companions. The real Catherine so treasured the little May basket and message Manjiro gave her (Chapter 24) that she kept them into her eighties.

Some incidents and characters are fictional. The characters of Jolly and Tom and their confrontations with Manjiro were invented to provide conflict and advance the story as well as to acknowledge the prejudice and ill will that Manjiro faced in a time and place where animosity toward Japan and its isolationist policies was in full flower.

By the time Manjiro returned home, Japan (known at the time as Nippon) had been living in isolation for 250 years.

CALENDAR METHOD

The old Japanese calendar used two methods. One was a complicated system involving the twelve animals of the Chinese zodiac (rat, ox, tiger, rabbit, dragon, snake, horse, sheep, monkey, hen, dog, and boar) and the five natural elements (earth, water, fire, wood, and metal). The other system was based on eras, which changed depending on the emperor in power, major events, and natural disasters. In the era system, a year is identified by the combination of the Japanese era name and the year number within the era. Our story starts in the twelfth year of Tempō, theYear of the Ox. The Tempō Era lasted from 1830 until 1844. The book concludes in the fifth year of Kaei, the Year of the Rat. The Kaei Era was from 1848 until 1854.

ENVIRONMENTAL NOTE

Like others of his generation, Manjiro probably could not have perceived that the whales he chased were being hunted to the brink of extinction. Even American author Herman Melville, who sailed on a whaling ship toward Japan at the same time Manjiro was sailing toward America, rejected the notion that whales could ever face extinction. He wrote in his book *Moby-Dick* that although "whales no longer haunt many grounds in former years abounding with them," they were just going to "some other and remoter strand." Or, he said, they could always go to the polar ice cap, where they could dive "under the glassy barriers, and, in a charmed circle of everlasting December, bid defiance to the pursuit of man."

Whales have not been able to defy the pursuit of man, who has hunted them to whatever "cape or promontory" they go to. Even after a moratorium on commercial hunting, whales continue to face many perils, including pollution, fishing nets and lines, military sonar, climate change, "scientific" whaling, and the possible renewal of commercial whaling.

Manjiro probably also could not have foreseen the near extinction of the bird that saved his life when he was ship-wrecked on Torishima: the short-tailed albatross. Primarily to satiate the appetite for exotic feathers (with which to decorate ladies' hats), the short-tailed albatross was hunted so recklessly that the population plummeted from millions to so few that they were considered extinct by the 1940s. A handful remained, probably only because some immature birds stay at sea all year, and so were unavailable for slaughter. Since the birds do not breed until at least ten years of age and lay only one egg per year, they have been slow to rebound. Now nesting on only two islands (one of which is the actively volcanic Torishima), the population has slowly increased to an extremely vulnerable twelve hundred birds.

GLOSSARY

JAPANESE WORDS/TERMS/PLACES

ahodori albatross, a large seabird, what Goemon calls a "fool bird," a short-tailed albatross, which once nested by the thousands on Torishima (Bird Island). Their numbers were once so greatly reduced by feather hunters that they were considered extinct. A small population now struggles to make a recovery.

Bushido the way of the samurai; a code of honor.

daimyo a powerful territorial lord. Each daimyo had a great many samurai in his service who swore allegiance to him according to the rules of Bushido.

Edo the former name of Tokyo during the Edo period.

fumi-e a likeness of Jesus or Mary upon which suspected Christians were made to step in order to prove they were not members of that religion.

geisha a professional female entertainer who performs traditional Japanese arts; typically dressed elegantly in a kimono.

Hagakure: The Book of the Samurai ("Hidden Leaves") a practical and spiritual guide for a warrior, from commentaries by Yamamoto Tsunetomo (eighteenth century).

hakama, haori traditional Japanese-style long, wide legged pants (*hakama*) and short jacket (*haori*).

Hiroshige (Ando Hiroshige, 1797–1858) painter and printmaker, known especially for his landscape prints.

Hitotsume-kozo a one-eyed boy or small creature found in Japanese folklore.

Itadakimasu "I humbly receive." Said before a meal to thank all those who had a part in it; also to acknowledge that living things have given their lives for the sustenance of human beings.

Izanami and Izanagi male and female deities and creators of Japan and its gods in Japanese mythology.

kago a method of transportation; a small platform on poles that rest on the shoulders of one or more bearers, used to carry members of the higher class.

kami divinities, natural forces, essence or life force in the Shinto religion.

kare-sansui dry landscape gardens in which raked sand and specially placed stones are used to suggest water, mountains, and other natural features.

katana a curved, single-edged blade traditionally worn by samurai, renowned for its sharpness and cutting ability. When it was worn with the *wakizashi* ("small sword"), the pair of swords together were called *daisho*, translating as "large and small."

kimono a traditional Japanese garment made of silk, tied around the waist with a sash (obi). It is usually ankle-length, with long, wide sleeves.

Kochi the capital city of Kochi Prefecture on the island of Shikoku. During the Meiji Restoration (shortly after Manjiro spent time there), the city became a center for promoting democratic and human rights movements.

Nagasaki the capital city of Nagasaki Prefecture on the island of Kyushu.

naginata a curved blade on the end of a long pole.

Namu Amida Butsu "Buddha of Infinite Light," phrase used by Buddhists as a chant or prayer.

nodachi a large, two-handed sword.

ojiisan "grandfather."

okachan "mother," or, more informal, "mama."

seppuku "belly slicing," when a samurai kills himself by cutting his belly open; a samurai would rather kill himself than bring shame and disgrace to his family name and lord.

shogun one of a line of military commanders who exercised absolute rule under the nominal leadership of the emperor until 1867; literally, "barbarian-expelling generalissimo."

sutra a Buddhist text or prayer.

tanto a knife or dagger.

tatami woven rice-straw matting used as a floor covering in traditional Japanese homes.

tenugui cotton cloth used as a headband or towel.

Urashima Taro a legendary character who is taken to an undersea kingdom by a grateful turtle.

wakizashi a sword of twelve to twenty-four inches, traditionally worn with the *katana* by samurai as a sidearm.

yukata a light-cotton summer kimono.

WHALING TERMS/PARTS OF A SHIP

ambergris a waxy brown or gray substance produced in the large intestine of a sperm whale and used as a fixative in perfumes.

baleen a plate inside the mouth of a toothless (baleen) whale, made of the same material as human fingernails or hair. Baleen was valued for its plasticity and was used like plastic is now: for buggy whips, umbrella ribs, carriage springs, skirt hoops, brushes, combs, fishing rods, and so on.

binnacle the stand on which the ship's compass is mounted.

blasted whale dead whale.

bulwark the sides of the ship that extend above the upper deck.

chanteys work songs.

chart the nautical counterpart of a map, showing land configurations, water depths, and other aids to navigation.

clumsy cleat a plank at the bow of a whaleboat, notched to take the whaleman's left thigh and steady him when throwing a harpoon.

deadeye a round or pear-shaped wooden disc with one or more holes through it used in the standing rigging to create tension in the shrouds.

dog watch the watches between 4 and 6 P.M. and 6 and 8 P.M.

doldrums an area of low pressure where the prevailing winds are calm, alternating with squalls and storms.

fathom a unit of length used for measuring the depth of water—there are six feet in a fathom.

footropes ropes stretched under the yards for crew members to stand on while loosing or furling the sails.

forecastle (fo'c'sle) sailors' living quarters at the head of the ship. A windowless space, it was typically dark, dank, and smelly.

futtock shrouds short lengths of rope supporting the top of a lower mast.

galley the ship's kitchen.

gam a social meeting of two or more whaling ships at sea.

green hand an untested, inexperienced sailor.

grog a drink of some parts rum and equal parts water.

gunnel (gunwale) the widened edge at the top of the side of a boat.

halyards ropes or lines used to hoist sails.

headsman the crewmember who steered the whaleboat when approaching the whale.

lobscouse a stew made of salted meat, vegetables (if available), and hardtack.

loggerhead a post in the stern of a whaleboat used to secure the harpoon rope.

luff to flap or flutter; said of a sail when losing wind (for instance, if sailing too close to the wind).

main yard the lowest yard on the mainmast, from which the mainsail is set.

marlin spike a polished tool tapered to a rounded or flattened point, six to twelve inches long or longer, used to separate the strands of a rope when splicing.

Mocha Dick an enormous albino sperm whale named for the island of Mocha, off the coast of Chile. Whalers tried and failed to kill him on numerous occasions. Some say he killed more than thirty men, attacked and damaged whaling ships and whaleboats, and served as the inspiration for Herman Melville's fictional giant white whale, Moby-Dick.

mutiny an open rebellion against a ship's captain.

Nantucket sleigh ride what a whaleboat is taken on when a harpooned whale attempts to flee, dragging the boat along with it, at speeds of over 20 mph.

plum duff a shipboard dessert of flour, lard, water, molasses, and raisins ("plums").

ratlines ropes or wooden steps made out of rope or wood attached to the shrouds to allow the sailors to climb into the rigging.

reef tackle tackle used to reef, or shorten, the sail area.

rigging ropes and chains that support and control the masts, spars, and sails of a vessel.

scrimshaw ornamental and pictorial items made from the teeth and bone of the whale.

sheet home to haul on the sheets (ropes or chains attached to the sails).

shorten sail to reduce the sail area.

shrouds sets of ropes or cables stretched from the masthead to the sides of a vessel to support the mast.

spar a long wooden timber or pole used as a yard or mast.

spermaceti a wax found inside the heads of sperm whales, used to make high-quality candles, soap, cosmetics, lubricants, lamp oil, and so on.

taffrail the rail around the stern of a ship.

thwart a plank across a boat upon which a rower might sit.

topgallant the mast above the topmast.

topgallant crosstrees timbers secured at the top of the topgallant mast upon which a sailor stood to watch for whales.

topsails sails set on a ship's topmast.

tow line a rope used in towing.

trice up to haul lines, blocks, or tackle out of the way and secure them while performing another task with sails or yards.

trim and make sail to adjust yards and sails and set further sail.

trypots/tryworks two cast iron pots, set into a furnace of brick, iron, and wood, in which oil was rendered from whale blubber.

yard a horizontal wooden boom (or spar) to which sail is firmly attached.

wigwag a whale pointer, used by lookouts on whale ships to indicate the direction of whale or whales.

SAILORS' LINGO

bleed the monkey to secretly remove liquor from a cask by making a small hole and sucking through a straw.

cross your bows to annoy you.

devil to pay and no pitch hot a predicament; derives from the job of sealing the outermost deck seam (the devil), which a sailor had to seal (pay) with pitch, a difficult and unpleasant task.

dickey run a short leave ashore.

half seas over half-drunk.

Jack Nastyface a derogatory nickname for a sailor who is disliked by his mates.

know the ropes to be experienced.

know which way the wind blows to see how things are going.

lay the whaling man's pay, which was delivered at the end of the journey and amounted to some predetermined fraction of the profits, minus the ship's and the crewman's expenses.

oppos pals, companions.

scuppered frustrated, defeated, killed. Scuppers are also a means to drain water off the deck.

shonkey of dubious quality; a shipmate who will drink but avoid paying his round.

slip his cable to die.

stow it shut up.

swallow the anchor to leave the sea or to retire.

three sheets to the wind drunk.

vast heaving stop or stop pulling my leg.

whistling psalms to the taffrail providing advice that will be ignored.

whistling up a wind to indulge in vain hopes of something.

MISCELLANEOUS

butter stinkers (*bata-kusai*) people who stink of butter, still used as a derogatory term in Japan for things obnoxiously Western.

calligraphy artistic handwriting.

mele a chant or song of the Hawaiian Islanders, often accompanied by a dance called the hula.

Sandwich Islands the historic name for the Hawaiian Islands.

taro a tropical plant grown as a vegetable.

BIBLIOGRAPHY AND SUGGESTED READING

Starred books are for younger readers

MANJIRO

Benfey, Christopher. *The Great Wave: Gilded Age Misfits, Japanese Eccentrics, and the Opening of Old Japan*. New York: Random House, 2003.

Bernard, Donald. *The Life and Times of John Manjiro*. New York: McGraw-Hill, 1992.

*Blumberg, Rhoda. *Shipwrecked! The True Adventures of a Japanese Boy*. New York: HarperCollins, 2001.

*Crofford, Emily. *Born in the Year of Courage*. Minneapolis: Carolrhoda, 1991.

Ibuse, Masuji. *Castaways: Two Short Novels*. Tokyo: Kodansha Int'l, 1987.

Kaneko, Hisakazu. *Manjiro, The Man Who Discovered America*. Boston: Houghton Mifflin, 1956.

Manjiro, John and Kawada Shoryo. *Drifting Toward the Southeast*. Translated by Junya Nagakuni and Junji Kitadai. New Bedford, Mass.: Spinner Publications, Inc., 2003.

Warriner, Emily V. *Voyager to Destiny*. Indianapolis: Bobbs-Merrill, 1956. (out of print)

WHALING

Ellis, Richard. *Men and Whales*. New York: Knopf, 1991.

*McKissack, Patricia C. and Fredrick L. *Black Hands, White Sails: The Story of African-American Whalers*. New York: Scholastic Press, 1999.

Melville, Herman. *Moby-Dick*. New York: Penguin Books, 1998. (originally published in 1851)

*Murphy, Jim. *Gone A-Whaling*. New York: Clarion Books, 1998.

Philbrick, Nathaniel. *In the Heart of the Sea: The Tragedy of the Whaleship Essex*. New York: Penguin Books, 2000.

*Philbrick, Nathaniel. *Revenge of the Whale: The True Story of the Whaleship Essex*. New York: G. P. Putnam's Sons, 2002.

*Sandler, Martin W. *Trapped in Ice! An Amazing True Whaling Adventure*. New York: Scholastic Nonfiction, 2006.

*Stanley, Diane. *The True Adventure of Daniel Hall*. New York: Dial Books for Young Readers, 1995.

The Story of Yankee Whaling. New York: American Heritage, 1959.

The Visual Encyclopedia of Nautical Terms Under Sail. New York: Crown Publishers Inc., 1978.

GOLD RUSH

The California Gold Rush, by the editors of American Heritage. New York: American Heritage, 1961.

*Blumberg, Rhoda. *The Great American Gold Rush*. New York: Bradbury Press, 1989.

*Stein, R. Conrad. *The California Gold Rush.* Chicago: Childrens Press, 1995.

SAMURAI

*Gaskin, Carol. *Secrets of the Samurai.* New York: Avon Books, 1991.

*Lewis, Brenda Ralph. *Growing Up in Samurai Japan.* London: Batsford Academic and Educational, 1981.

*Macdonald, Fiona. *How to Be a Samurai Warrior.* Washington, D.C.: National Geographic, 2005.

*Schomp, Virginia. *Japan in the Days of the Samurai.* New York: Benchmark Books, 2002.

Tsuentomo, Yamamoto. *Hagakure: The Art of the Samurai.* Translated by Bruce Steben. London: Duncan Baird, 2008.

Tsunetomo, Yamamoto. *Hagakure: The Book of the Samurai.* Translated by William Scott Wilson. Tokyo: Kodansha, Int'l., 1979.

JAPAN

*Blumberg, Rhoda. *Commodore Perry in the Land of the Shogun.* New York: Lothrop, Lee and Shepard Books, 1985.

Dunn, Charles James. *Everyday Life in Traditional Japan.* London: Putnam, 1969.

Hanley, Susan B. *Everyday Things in Premodern Japan: The Hidden Legacy of Material Culture.* Berkeley: University of California Press, 1997.

Matsunosuke, Nishiyama. *Edo Culture: Daily Life and Diversions in Urban Japan, 1600–1868.* Translated and edited by Gerald Groemer. Honolulu: University of Hawai'i Press, 1997.

ACKNOWLEDGMENTS

I would like to extend grateful acknowledgments to: Eri Fujieda, friend and translator, and the hospitable Fujieda family; Hiromi Tanaka, Arthur Davis, and friends of the Welcome John Mung Society in Tosashimizu; Jean Walsh, who introduced me to the story; Carolyn Longworth of the Millicent Library in Fairhaven; kind librarians at the New Bedford Whaling Museum research library; tall ship expert and exceptionally tall Bob Bruce; my erudite writing group; my patient husband and inspirational children; my remarkable agent, Stephen Fraser, who is a great-great-great-grandson of Nathaniel Bowditch (author of *The New American Practical Navigator*); and everyone at Abrams who worked on this book, especially Howard Reeves, the oracle.

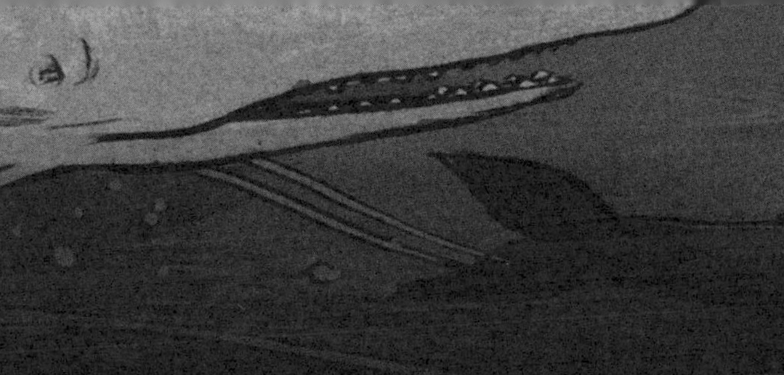

ABOUT THE AUTHOR

Margi Preus is a children's book author and playwright. Her other books include *Shadow on the Mountain* and *West of the Moon*. She came upon the story of Manjiro while researching another subject and was attracted by the true story of a courageous boy and an unlikely and ultimately world-changing friendship. Preus lives in Duluth, Minnesota, where she keeps a weather eye out for whales in Lake Superior.

This book was designed and art directed by Chad W. Beckerman. The text is set in 12-point Adobe Jenson, a typeface originally drawn by Nicolas Jenson. Its Roman styles are based on a Venetian old-style text face created in 1470. The modern version used in this book was designed by Robert Slimbach. The display font is Samurai.

KEEP READING FOR A SNEAK PEEK AT

MARGI PREUS' NEXT BOOK!

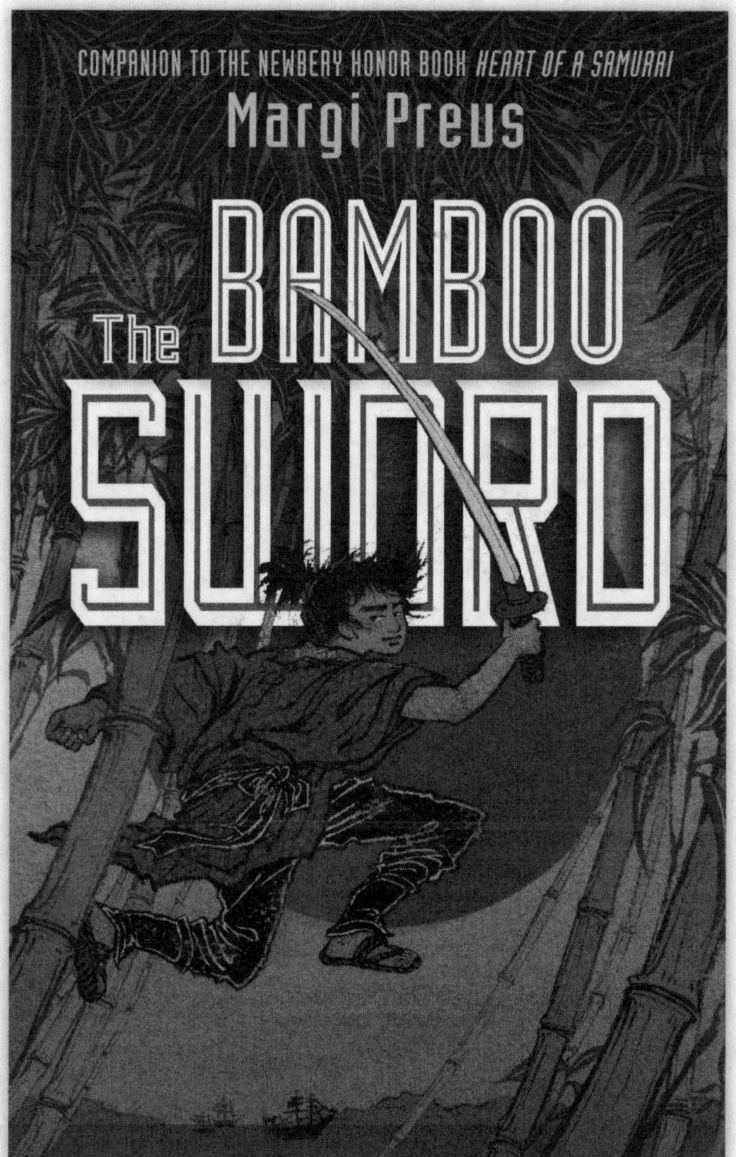
COMPANION TO THE NEWBERY HONOR BOOK *HEART OF A SAMURAI*
Margi Preus
The BAMBOO SWORD

BLACK DRAGONS BELCHING SMOKE

3rd Day of the 6th Month of the 6th Year of the Era of Long Happiness (July 8, 1853)

Yoshi was a leaf, spinning in the summer breeze. He was water running over stones. He was the thin, free air.

Or at least that was what he tried to be. But, really, he was just Yoshi, spinning, lunging, twisting, and slashing. The sword he imagined flashing in his hands was only a length of bamboo. His blade did not exactly flash, but it was at least burnished by the early morning sunlight.

He kept his heels slightly off the ground so as to move quickly, but he could never quite capture the graceful, gliding motions of the teacher. No matter how much he practiced, he still felt awkward. His slow moves weren't smooth enough, his fast moves not quick enough. *More practice,* he told himself.

Under the flickering green leaves, with the sound of the rushing brook in his ears, Yoshi started again. But something, he wasn't sure what, made him drop his arm, stand still, and listen.

Except for the brook and the silvery call of a bird, it was quiet. A familiar quiet, old as these hills and the nearby temple, old as the silent stone Buddha who watched him at his sword practice. But now he noticed that there *was* a sound, a kind of dull thumping, as if his heart were beating somewhere outside his body. It was so faint that it was almost not a sound.

He walked to the rocky outcropping that overlooked the village and the bay beyond. A humid haze hung over the valley, made thicker by the smoke from cooking fires. In the village, women were just now rising to begin making their families' breakfasts. He slid his hand into the fold of his sleeve and felt the cold rice ball wrapped in a radish leaf.

Should he eat some? Or save it? He was hungry now, so perhaps now would be a good time. But he would be hungry later, too, and it was painful to watch the other boys eat while he had nothing. He pulled his hand away. He could wait.

Beyond the village, the blue water of the bay winked in the early morning sun. Boats were just leaving the harbor for a day of fishing, their sails bright against the dark hills. Every day the water in the bay looked different: black under glowering clouds, or blue as the daimyo's silk kimono. Some days it moved as if it were alive, rippling like a horse's flank.

Why was it that the water could change every day, but absolutely nothing else ever did? The village below—its thatched roofs and bamboo fences, the skinny stray dogs that trotted along the dirt roads—it had all been like this for hundreds of years and would be forever more, as far as Yoshi could tell. These ancient hills and the temples hidden in them had stood for thousands of years, and probably would for thousands more.

And yet, this morning, something seemed different. It was as if everything—the village, the hills beyond, the early morning mist and the smoke from cooking fires, the last reverberation of the temple bell, even the water in the bay—everything seemed to be holding its breath.

The only sound was the steady thumping Yoshi had noticed earlier, and which had grown closer. Yoshi now recognized it as a runner's soft, thudding footfall. Next the runner himself appeared, a man dressed in a short kimono and a lacquer hat who raced along the path toward the daimyo's dwelling place. The man glanced at Yoshi as he ran past. "You'd better hang on to your 'sword,' little 'samurai,'" he panted.

"What?" Yoshi said. "Why?"

"In the bay!" the man called over his shoulder. "Black dragons belching smoke!"

What a crazy person! Yoshi thought, but when he turned back to glance at the valley one more time, he saw something he had not noticed before. Far down the bay, toward the ocean, puffs of black smoke rose into the air.

THROWING ROCKS AT THE SUN

On the way to Hideki's dojo, Yoshi carried the slippers his young master would wear later in his indoor classes, and an extra pair of wooden clogs in case of wet weather. He walked slightly behind and to the side of Hideki. On the other side was the umbrella bearer, Jun, who shielded the young samurai's head from the hot sun.

Hideki had turned fifteen the previous year, and he now wore the samurai's daisho: the two swords, one long and one short. As they walked along the dirt road to the school, Hideki clicked his fingers against the hilt of his katana, something he shouldn't do. Perhaps he was still having trouble getting used to the swords, Yoshi thought.

Yoshi knew he should not look left or right but instead keep his eyes straight ahead. Still, he couldn't help craning his neck to see if anything unusual was happening.

"What is it, Yoshitaro?" Hideki asked kindly, using Yoshi's full name. "Are you looking for something?"

"Please excuse my foolishness," Yoshi said, lowering his

might be a samurai. But even if he really were, he would not shoot dogs!

"In this next exercise, we will say that the two opponents are in the following positions," the sword master was saying. Yoshi turned his attention to him.

Behind Yoshi, Jun yawned and said, "Time for a nap!" He stretched out under a ginkgo tree. "How about you?"

"Maybe in a bit," Yoshi said.

"Don't get any big ideas, Yoshitaro-san," Jun teased. "You'll never be a bushi, you know, no matter how much you eavesdrop on their lessons."

"I know, but . . ." Yoshi bit his tongue and turned his attention back to the instructor, who was showing how to knock an opponent's sword away. The teacher made it look easy, demonstrating with one of the students.

"You're like the boy who throws rocks at the sun," Jun joked.

"Uh-huh," Yoshi said absently. The instructor was demonstrating another move, using a real blade. Yoshi loved to watch the teacher's graceful moves, the curving lines, the smooth, perfect steel—the way man and sword became one fluid, lethal dancer.

Later, alone in the forest, Yoshi would practice what he had observed. He would try to move in the teacher's slow, sure, meditative way, then dart, fast as a snake, to wound his imaginary opponent.

"You're funny," Jun said. "You're the only one watching. Even his students don't pay attention to him."

It was true. The students who were waiting their turns lolled in the heat, their heads drooping. Some of them who waited outside were dozing under the trees, the shade hiding their closed eyes.

"They're all bored, " Jun said. "What do they need to learn this for, anyway? There hasn't been a war for hundreds of years."

"I suppose you're right," Yoshi replied. "But what if there *was* one?"

"A war with whom?" Jun said. "The shogun has complete power. He keeps the families of the lords in Edo, as if they were hostages, so they can't rebel. The only time samurai ever use their swords is to test their sharpness on corpses. Or on poor peasants like us."

"What if the barbarians from the West should come?" Yoshi said.

Jun scoffed. "Barbarians! If they come, our warriors will run them through—one, two, three!" He slapped his hands together as if cleaning them off. "The things you think! Why do you waste your time with such worry?" He closed his eyes.

Everything Jun said was true. Yoshi and Jun would never

carry swords, never put on battle armor, never ride a horse into war, even if there was one. Still, he couldn't help but watch the sword master's graceful movements, mentally imitating them, while wondering why *did* he waste his time learning things he could never use? It was like Jun said, as senseless as throwing rocks at the sun.

As he pondered this, a horse and rider thundered into the courtyard. The rider glanced around and, apparently deciding that Kitsune was the highest-ranked samurai there, dismounted, ran to him, and, bowing, gasped his breathless message: "Foreign ships in the harbor—black ships that move without sails! Alien ships of fire! The country is about to be invaded by a hundred thousand white devils! All samurai are to prepare for battle!"

MARGI PREUS
WEST OF THE MOON
NEW YORK TIMES BESTSELLING AUTHOR AND NEWBURY HONOR WINNER

KEEP READING!

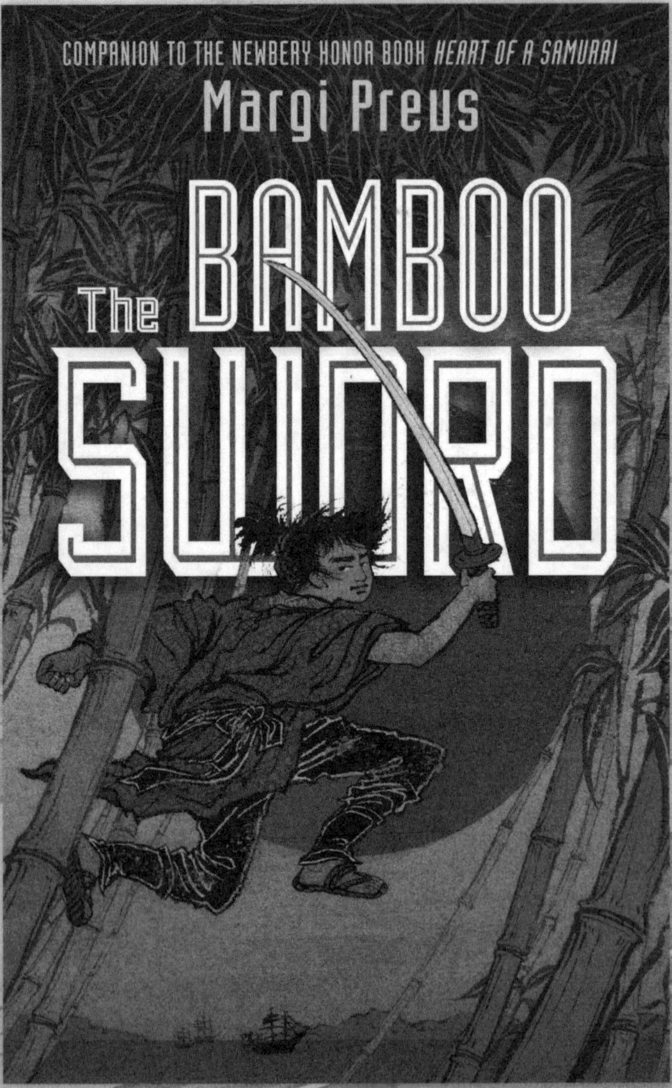